Samuel French Acting Edition

Something Fishy

by Marcia Kash &
Douglas E. Hughes

I0591907

‖ SAMUEL FRENCH ‖

SAMUELFRENCH.COM   SAMUELFRENCH.CO.UK

FOR PRODUCTION ENQUIRIES

UNITED STATES AND CANADA
Info@SamuelFrench.com
1-866-598-8449

UNITED KINGDOM AND EUROPE
Plays@SamuelFrench.co.uk
020-7255-4302

Each title is subject to availability from Samuel French, depending
upon country of performance. Please be aware that *SOMETHING
FISHY* may not be licensed by Samuel French in your territory.
Professional and amateur producers should contact the nearest Samuel
French office or licensing partner to verify availability.

MUSIC USE NOTE

Licensees are solely responsible for obtaining formal written permission from copyright owners to use copyrighted music in the performance of this play and are strongly cautioned to do so. If no such permission is obtained by the licensee, then the licensee must use only original music that the licensee owns and controls. Licensees are solely responsible and liable for all music clearances and shall indemnify the copyright owners of the play(s) and their licensing agent, Samuel French, against any costs, expenses, losses and liabilities arising from the use of music by licensees. Please contact the appropriate music licensing authority in your territory for the rights to any incidental music.

IMPORTANT BILLING AND CREDIT REQUIREMENTS

If you have obtained performance rights to this title, please refer to your licensing agreement for important billing and credit requirements.

SOMETHING FISHY was commissioned by Lighthouse Festival Theatre in Port Dover, Ontario, Canada and received its premiere production there on June 30, 2016. The production was directed by Marcia Kash, with set designs by Bill Chesney, costumes by Alex Amini, and lighting by Renee Brode. The stage manager was Kevin Olson, and the assistant stage manager was Erika Morey. The cast was as follows:

ACTOR 1 . . . . Brad Rudy

ACTOR 2 . . . . Kaitlyn Riordan

ACTOR 3 . . . . Andrea Risk

ACTOR 4 . . . . Nigel Bennett

ACTOR 5 . . . . Matt Gorman

CHARACTERS

Something Fishy has fourteen characters who are designed to be played by five actors. The breakdown is as follows:

ACTOR 1

RAYMOND BREAM – Mid-forties to mid-fifties; a successful career politician running for office; handsome and charismatic.

ROLAND BREAM – Raymond's identical twin brother; an actor in the Port Pilchard Players (PPP); a shaggy, unkempt but likeable loser.

DR. ZINGEL – Sixtyish; a stereotypical German scientist in a lab coat and Einstein hair.

ACTOR 2

LORENA – Late thirties; Raymond's campaign manager; attractive, Puerto Rican, speaks English fluently but with a pronounced accent.

MOLLY – Thirties; stage manager for the PPP; quintessential stage manager type: overworked, undervalued, but good at her job.

JUDY – Fortyish; one of the PPP actors; opinionated, very full of herself, has an air of superiority about her.

ACTOR 3

PENELOPE – Fifties; a southern belle and artistic director of the PPP; warm, outgoing, a mother-hen.

MANDY – Older than Penelope but trying desperately to look twenty-five years younger; an actor in the company; vain, voluptuous, over-sexed.

WEEVER – Fifty to sixty; an unscrupulous, power-hungry, buttoned-up politician and Bream's opponent in the election.

ACTOR 4

GILL – Late forties to fifties; Weever's hatchet man, a hard-boiled, old-school back-room political operative.

COLIN – Fifties; an affable, enthusiastic actor in the PPP.

ACTOR 5

SHARKEY – Thirties; Gill's partner in crime, new to the political game but an avid pupil.

WHITING – Late twenties; cub reporter for a right-wing news website, tenacious, ambitious, cynical.

CLARK – Thirties; another PPP stalwart, mild-mannered, good-natured, loyal friend of Colin's.

AUTHOR'S NOTES

The stage directions in this play are essential to its understanding. Ignore them at your peril!

Although the published version is set in the United States, we recognize that for the purposes of productions abroad, you may wish to set it in another country (for example the premiere production was set in Canada), requiring some simple changes. A template of the portions of the script that will need to be altered for this purpose can be found at the back of the script. These are the only changes permitted.

ACT ONE

(Setting: Backstage area of the Community Center auditorium in Port Pilchard, Ohio, a small town on the shores of Lake Erie.)

(There are three walls upstage forming the back of the set of The Vicar's Knickers, *a British farce being produced by The Port Pilchard Players, an amateur theatre company.)*

(There are doors on each of these walls, one upstage center, one upstage right, and one upstage left. Upstage left is a large quick-change booth with curtains. Left and right of the upstage center door are props tables with a variety of props set on them. Downstage right is the exit to the kitchen and dressing rooms. Downstage left is an emergency door leading to the alley outside. Upstage right there is a rolling rack with a host of different costumes hanging on it, and scattered about are a few chairs. There are some practical backstage lights rigged up and assorted paraphernalia belonging to the community center tucked in the corners, such as a Rotary sign, some flagpoles belonging to the Lions Club, folded up banquet tables, gym mats, yoga props, and the like.)

(The three doors on the Vicar's Knickers *set are closed at all times unless otherwise specified.)*

(The time is the present. It is about 1:30 p.m. on a Saturday afternoon in November, three days before the Presidential election.)

(Lights come up on a rehearsal for The Vicar's Knickers, *which is set in London in the 1950s.)*

(Seated in one of the chairs stage right is **CLARK**, *dressed as a British aristocrat. He's busy studying his script, mouthing his lines to himself as he reads his cues.* **COLIN**, *wearing a doctor's lab coat, stethoscope, and sporting a fake mustache, stands waiting for his entrance at the stage left door.)*

*(***ROLAND**, *with long straggly hair and a beard and dressed in a vicar's cassock and hat, sits in a chair near the upstage center entrance, scrolling on his phone. From onstage we hear the voices of two of the troupe's actors,* **JUDY**, *playing the femme fatale and speaking in a bad British accent, and* **MANDY**, *playing a maid, speaking with an equally bad Italian accent.)*

(Throughout the play, much of the dialogue coming from characters who are offstage [i.e. from the dressing rooms, over the Tannoy, or from the stage or front of house area] will need to be pre-recorded. All such dialogue will be indicated in italics.)

MANDY. *(Offstage.)* Milady, the Vicar is 'ere to see you about-a de bowl.

JUDY. *(Offstage.)* The bowl? What bowl?

MANDY. *(Offstage.)* Not-a de bowl, de *bowl*. De fancy dress-a bowl.

JUDY. *(Offstage.)* Oh, the BALL! Of course! Oh, bugger the Vicar and bugger the ball!

MANDY. *(Offstage.)* Shall I show him in?

JUDY. *(Offstage.)* Yes.

*(**MANDY** opens the door to come back "offstage.")*

(Offstage.) NO!

*(**MANDY** slams the door shut.)*

(Offstage.) Offer him some lunch. Tell him I'm... indisposed. I'll be with him as soon as I can manage.

MANDY. *(Offstage.)* Very good, Milady.

*(**MANDY**, dressed as a frumpy Italian cleaning lady, exits through the upstage center door and closes it. Under the following dialogue she checks her watch, does a quick calculation, and hustles off toward the dressing rooms downstage right, undoing her costume and swanning off sexily.)*

JUDY. *(Offstage.)* That bloody Vicar. He always shows up at the most inconvenient times.

*(Opening the upstage left door and ushering **COLIN** onstage.)*

Alright darling, you can come out of the closet now.

(She closes the door. There is a sound of a big smoochy kiss.)

COLIN. *(Offstage.)* Oh darling, you look ravishing.

JUDY. *(Offstage.)* We've got to be quick. I've got an appointment with the Vicar.

COLIN. *(Offstage.)* The Vicar? He never struck me as the type.

JUDY. Oh you idiot! Not that kind of appointment.

COLIN. *(Offstage.)* Look, there's a car pulling up the drive.

JUDY. *(Offstage.)* Good lord! It's my husband!

COLIN. *(Offstage.)* Your husband? But you said he was in Constantinople.

JUDY. *(Offstage.)* Istanbul, darling. That's what his telegram said. But it must have been a ruse. I knew he was on to us. If he finds you here he'll kill you!

COLIN. *(Offstage.)* I've got to get out of here.

(**CLARK** *looks up, sees* **ROLAND** *engrossed on his phone, and snaps his fingers at him. No response.*)

CLARK. *(Whispering.)* Psst. Roland!

(**ROLAND** *looks up and* **CLARK** *gestures toward the stage.*)

JUDY. *(Offstage.)* Quick! Go into the bedroom –

COLIN. *(Offstage.)* The bedroom? This is hardly the time.

(**ROLAND** *rises, stretches, crosses to the upstage center door, still paging through his phone as he waits for his cue.*)

JUDY. *(Offstage.)* Shut up and listen. There's a rack of costumes in there for the fancy dress ball we're hosting for the local orphanage this weekend. Go in there and disguise yourself.

COLIN. *(Offstage.)* As what?

JUDY. *(Offstage.)* It doesn't matter – just throw something on.

COLIN. *(Offstage.)* Right. Stall him for as long as you can!

(**COLIN** *comes flying in through the door upstage right. He pulls off his doctor's coat, stethoscope, and pants and drops them on the floor as he crosses to the quick-change booth and disappears inside.* **ROLAND** *suddenly sees something on his phone that alarms him. Beat.*)

JUDY. *(Offstage, improvising.)* Ummmmmmmmm... Did I hear a knock?

(Under her breath.) Oh for God's sake!

(Another beat.)

(Aloud.) Would that be Vicar Knickerson, by chance?

MOLLY. *(Over the Tannoy.)* Roland! That's your cue!

(**ROLAND** *is transfixed by what he sees on his phone.* **COLIN** *sticks his head out of the quick-change booth.*)

COLIN. Roland!

ROLAND. *(Loudly.)* OH MY GOD!

> **(CLARK,** *startled, drops his script in terror,* **JUDY** *opens the upstage right door and looks in.)*

JUDY. *(Angrily, indicating for him to come in.)* Roland!

ROLAND. *(Looking up, horrified.)* TERRORISTS!

JUDY. What?

> *(All the actors – both onstage and off – lose their accents and speak in their normal voices.)*

What are you talking about?

CLARK. *(Overlapping.)* What's happened?

COLIN. Terrorists?

ROLAND. Terrorists! Right here in downtown Port Pilchard! Check it out!

> **(COLIN** *comes out of the quick-change booth dressed in boxers, a sleeveless t-shirt, dress shoes, and socks with suspenders, as well as a woman's wig and an enormous pair of fake boobs. His eyes are glued to his phone.)*

CLARK. *(Looking up at* **COLIN***'s ensemble.)* Nice outfit, Colin.

COLIN. It will be, if I ever manage to get it all on! It's opening night tonight, and I've never got through this damn quick-change once!

> *(Referring to what he's reading on his phone.)*

This is incredible.

> **(JUDY** *and* **CLARK** *pull out their phones. They all join* **ROLAND** *at center and begin searching.)*

MOLLY. *(Over the Tannoy.)* What's going on? Where did everybody go? HEY!

COLIN. *(Reading his phone.)* "The downtown core of Port Pilchard is in lockdown at this hour due to a bomb threat issued at the local town hall where Congressman Raymond Bream was scheduled to deliver an important campaign speech this afternoon. Just three days before the election, Congressman Bream has overtaken President Weever in the polls in their race to the White House."

CLARK. Look at this – there's an armored personnel carrier in front of the post office!

(**PENELOPE WITHERSPOON,** *the director of the Port Pilchard Players, comes striding in through the upstage center door. She's wearing a lanyard with an ID card on it and is carrying a handful more.*)

PENELOPE. Sorry everyone, but...

(*They all speak at once, talking over each other.*)

COLIN. There's been a bomb go off!

JUDY. ISIS has taken over Port Pilchard!

ROLAND. They've locked down the whole town!

PENELOPE. (*Shouting them down.*) Calm down, calm down. Everything's fine. There aren't any terrorists. Someone just called in a bomb threat at the town hall. It's probably just a hoax.

CLARK. Looks like someone doesn't want your brother to make his speech, Roland.

PENELOPE. That's exactly what the authorities think.

COLIN. What was he gonna say anyway?

ROLAND. Don't ask me.

CLARK. What a shame. I was hoping he had some good news for poor Port Pilchard.

PENELOPE. Oh, the speech hasn't been cancelled. It will go on as scheduled; but for obvious reasons, there's going to be a change of venue...

COLIN. Change of venue? To where?

CLARK. The only other place in town big enough to handle a crowd like that...would be here at the community center.

PENELOPE. That's right.

COLIN. He's doing his speech *here*?

JUDY. You mean HERE here?

PENELOPE. *(Brightly.)* Exactly!

JUDY. But what about our dress rehearsal?

COLIN. What about our opening night?

PENELOPE. Don't worry, everything will go ahead as planned. I've spoken with the congressman's people and they assure me that they will be all done well before five o'clock, which gives us plenty of time to finish the dress rehearsal before the curtain tonight.

> *(Holding up the ID cards and passing them out.)*

Now, you're each going to need one of these to get in and out of the building. Security is checking them so don't lose them, whatever you do.

CLARK. *(Putting it on over his head with pride.)* Ooh look, we're special.

PENELOPE. Where's Mandy?

ROLAND. I think she's gone for a quickie with Boo Radley.

PENELOPE. Who?

ROLAND. You know, that kid who works the lights; the one with the pizza face and the mullet.

CLARK. Well, it's official. She's now worked her way through the entire company.

COLIN. *(Indignantly.)* Present company excluded.

JUDY. That's not what we heard, Colin.

PENELOPE. *(Horrified.)* Wait a minute – Percy? For heaven's sake, he's just a child!

> *(From the dressing room area there is a loud moan of ecstasy.)*

ROLAND. Sounds like he's just become a man.

> (**ROLAND** *chuckles. There are general expressions of dismay from the others.*)

PENELOPE. *(Handing a lanyard to* **JUDY.***)* Do me a favor and make sure she gets this, will you darling?

MOLLY. *(Over the Tannoy.) Penelope, are you there?*

PENELOPE. *(Calling.)* Yes, Molly.

MOLLY. *(Over the Tannoy.) There are two guys here wearing sunglasses and earpieces who want to talk to you.*

PENELOPE. *(Calling.)* On my way.

> *(To the others.)* Right. We'll see you all back here at five o'clock to finish off the run-through.

JUDY. There's not going to be enough time! We've got all of scene two to get through.

COLIN. And I've still got to practice that quick-change.

PENELOPE. We'll have plenty of time, don't you worry. The play's in great shape as it is. I couldn't have hoped for a better cast. You're all so wonderful in it. I only wish Crispian Postlethwaite and Roger Dickey-Dennis could see what we've done with their play.

ROLAND. *(Under his breath.)* Done *to* it, you mean.

> *(She starts for the door.)*

PENELOPE. Oh and Roland – don't forget. You promised to go to the barber.

ROLAND. Yeah, sure.

> *(She exits.)*

JUDY. About time, too.

ROLAND. What, you got something against hairy clergymen?

JUDY. Roland, be reasonable; we can't have our vicar looking like Jesus Christ. It's sacrilegious.

ROLAND. Don't get your knickers in a twist, I'm going.

> *(He starts out the upstage center door, muttering.)*

Forgive them Father, for they know not what they do.

(He exits and closes the door. Throughout the following, **COLIN** *changes back into his doctor's outfit, leaving his disguise in the quick-change booth.)*

JUDY. *(Gesturing towards Roland's exit.)* And off he goes, in full costume and makeup. What a hot mess. I told Penelope not to give him the role.

COLIN. Oh come on Judy, he's a damn good actor.

JUDY. He's a liability.

CLARK. *(Paging through his phone.)* Hey, check this out. Someone's posted a photo of our parking lot. It's packed with media trucks. Look, CNN! Exciting, isn't it?

JUDY. Exciting? It's a disaster!

COLIN. It *could* have been a disaster. Imagine if it had been a real bomb. It might have killed our candidate!

JUDY. I'm not talking about the stupid election. I'm talking about the opening night of *The Vicar's Knickers*!

COLIN. *(Archly.)* Of course. Silly me. I really must get my priorities straight.

JUDY. *(Oblivious to* **COLIN***'s sarcasm.)* I finally get a decent role and look what happens! I mean, how can anyone expect me to carry the show when we're so woefully under-rehearsed?

CLARK. I'm sorry, did you just say "carry the show"? You realize the play is called "The *Vicar's* Knickers," don't you?

JUDY. Yes – and considering that I've had to memorize all of the Vicar's lines, I'd say I'm the one who's holding this whole show together!

COLIN. You didn't have to go to those lengths, Judy. Roland's been fine.

CLARK. Yes, he's been very well-behaved.

JUDY. So far.

CLARK. Oh come on, be fair. Since Penelope laid down the law, he hasn't touched a drop.

JUDY. That we know of. But you watch. It's only a matter of time before he falls off the wagon. Again.

CLARK. Still, I think memorizing all of his dialogue is a bit excessive.

JUDY. It's self-preservation, pure and simple. Remember that fiasco in *The Count of Monte Cristo*?

COLIN. Don't remind me.

JUDY. When Penelope got the bright idea of sticking an earpiece in his ear so she could feed him the lines that he was too drunk to remember?

COLIN. *(Laughing.)* And the local taxi company's frequency kept cutting in...

CLARK. *(Laughing as well.)* And instead of his speech at the end of Act Two, poor Roland started dispatching cabs all over town.

> *(Beat.)*

COLIN. *(Changing the subject.)* Amazing when you think about it.

JUDY. What is?

COLIN. That Roland and Raymond Bream are brothers.

CLARK. Not just brothers – twins! Who would have thought that two people with identical DNA could be such polar opposites?

COLIN. No kidding. Roland can't hold down a job...

CLARK. ...And on Tuesday, Raymond's going to become our next president.

JUDY. Heaven forfend.

CLARK. *(In disbelief.)* Don't tell me you're voting for Weever, Judy.

JUDY. Well I'm certainly not voting for Raymond Bream. The man's insane! Have you seen his energy plan?

COLIN. What about it?

JUDY. Oh Colin, you don't actually think you can run a car on a tank full of dead fish, do you?

CLARK. It's not dead fish; it's refined perch oil, mixed with ethanol and a few other ingredients – hence the name: The Perch-oil Urea *[you-REE-ah]* –fication process.

JUDY. P.U. for short. Just what we need – something that makes your car smell like a tuna fish sandwich.

CLARK. It doesn't make your car smell like a tuna fish sandwich. It's a clean-burning fuel, and it's odorless.

JUDY. Not according to the President's commercials. They spell it right out for you – "P.U. – It Stinks."

COLIN. *(Sarcastically.)* And as we all know, if it's in one of Weever's commercials, it must be true!

CLARK. You're not seriously going to vote for those idiots, are you, Judy?

JUDY. It beats the alternative.

COLIN. How can you say that? You mean you actually support those racist, homophobic crooks?

JUDY. *(Derisively.)* Oh, here we go...

COLIN. These last four years under Weever have been a nightmare. The Weevils have broken every promise they made – to take care of the little guy, to create jobs, to clean up the corruption in Washington. And what did they give us instead? Tax cuts for the rich, no health care for the poor, and the most inept, ethically challenged government in history. It's a miracle they haven't managed to start World War III. And as for jobs, thanks to Weever, we now have the highest unemployment figures since the Great Depression!

JUDY. Oh that's just a load of left-wing propaganda. It's all fake news and you know it.

COLIN. Oh yeah? Try selling that to all those poor people who used to work at the Port Pilchard Power Plant. Anyway, you can vote for whoever you want. It's not gonna matter. As far as this district is concerned, Bream's a shoo-in.

JUDY. Just shows you how gullible the electorate can be. "The Bream Team." If Raymond Bream wins we're going to be the only country in the world run by a crazy person.

COLIN. Tell that to the North Koreans.

JUDY. *(Getting up.)* Anyway, I don't have time to stand around arguing politics with you two. I've got things to do. We still have an opening night party to prepare for.

CLARK. Oh, are you making your famous guacamole?

JUDY. *(Proudly.)* Don't I always?

COLIN. *(Feigning enthusiasm.)* Mmmm. Can't wait.

> (**JUDY** *exits.* **COLIN** *and* **CLARK** *pull faces. Judy's guacamole is horrible.*)

CLARK. Wow. We're on the eve of the most important election this country has seen in decades, and all she can think about is her guacamole.

COLIN. I just don't get it. How do normally sentient human beings fall for Weever's lies?

CLARK. It's their messaging. Say what you want about this government, but when it comes to marketing they're geniuses. Look at that commercial – the one with the Subaru.

COLIN. *(Chuckling.)* Oh yeah, that car sputtering to a halt in the middle of the road. And all those cats coming out and licking the tailpipe.

(Announcer voice.) "P.U: It sure smells fishy to us."

COLIN & CLARK. Meow!

> *(They laugh.)*

CLARK. And it's on the air every five minutes. The Weevils must be spending a fortune on those ads.

COLIN. They're running scared. They'll say anything at this point to stop Bream from getting elected. I bet they were the ones who called in that bomb threat at the town hall. That sort of move has Weever written all over it.

CLARK. Do you think they'd go that far?

COLIN. Damn right I do. These bozos will do anything to stay in power.

CLARK. *(A beat.)* Hey, do you think with all the media here that some of them might stay for the show?

COLIN. Don't get your hopes up.

CLARK. We could get reviewed by the *New York Times*!

COLIN. I don't know about the *New York Times*, but if you don't get those lines down by tonight, the *Port Pilchard Post* is going to tear you to ribbons.

CLARK. Speaking of which, do you think you could run through a couple of scenes with me?

COLIN. If you'll help me with my quick-change.

> *(He crosses to the props table to get a stopwatch.)*

CLARK. Well, if you're looking for someone to do up your bra strap, I'm not your guy.

COLIN. I just need you to time me! Here –

> *(Handing **CLARK** the stopwatch.)*

Just give me a minute to organize my stuff.

> *(He goes into the quick-change booth as **MOLLY**, the stage manager, enters upstage right carrying a box of programs.)*

CLARK. Hey Molly. What have you got there?

MOLLY. Programs. They just arrived.

CLARK. *(Excited.)* Ooh, let me see!

> *(He puts down the stopwatch, takes the box from **MOLLY** and sets it on a chair. **MOLLY**'s phone dings as **CLARK** looks in the box.)*

What happened in here? It looks like they've been hit by a tornado.

MOLLY. *(Typing on her phone.)* That was the Secret Service. They were checking for plastic explosives.

> *(She exits the way she came. **CLARK** flips through one of the programs and snorts in surprise.)*

CLARK. Hey Colin!

(**COLIN** *comes out from the booth.*)

COLIN. Yeah.

CLARK. Check this out.

(He holds out the program. **COLIN** *squints.)*

COLIN. Who the hell is that?

CLARK. Mandy.

COLIN. *(Laughs.)* Are you kidding me? Where did she find that? Her high school yearbook?

CLARK. How old do you think she really is?

COLIN. Well, she's been thirty-nine for as long as I've known her.

CLARK. *(Incredulous.)* Thirty-nine?

COLIN. Well, it makes sense if you do the math.

CLARK. The math?

COLIN. Yeah, the facelift was what, fourteen years ago, the butt job was five and those boobs aren't a day over twenty.

> (**MANDY** *enters from the dressing room, dressed in a low-cut robe showing lots of cleavage. Her hair is wrapped up turban-style in a towel. She looks very glamorous.)*

CLARK. *(Seeing* **MANDY** *and covering.)* Hey, Mandy!

> (**COLIN** *gulps and turns to her with a big smile.* **COLIN** *and* **CLARK** *quickly drop the program on one of the props tables.)*

COLIN. Mandy.

MANDY. Have you guys heard the latest?

COLIN. What now?

MANDY. Pussy Creek!

CLARK. I beg your pardon?

MANDY. You know. Pussy Creek. My home town.

COLIN. You're kidding, right?

MANDY. No, it's true. I'm a native Pussy Creeker.

COLIN. Isn't there a cream for that?

CLARK. Anyway, what happened in Pussy Creek?

MANDY. Raymond Bream just saved someone's life in the Dunkin' Donuts there.

CLARK & COLIN. What?

(They check their phones.)

MANDY. Yeah, he went into the men's room and found some guy lying on the floor unconscious, gave him the kiss of life. And just think – he's going to be here any minute! Maybe I should play dead and he can give *me* the kiss of life.

(Excited.)

Ooh, better go freshen up.

*(She exits into the dressing room area. **COLIN** and **CLARK** watch her go.)*

COLIN. Wow. Where does she find the energy?

CLARK. Must be something in the water in Pussy Creek.

COLIN. Come on Clarkie. Help me do this quick-change. I've got exactly forty-five seconds.

CLARK. *(Fiddling with the stopwatch.)* Right. Forty-five seconds to transform from doctor to dowager.

COLIN. Hit start when you hear my exit line.

(He checks himself to make sure he's got everything, then heads out onto the stage through the door upstage left and closes it.)

CLARK. Ready when you are.

COLIN. OK, here goes...

(Offstage, in character, as before.) Right! Stall him for as long as you can!

(He comes flying through the door upstage right, slams it shut, and rushes to the quick-change booth, leaving a trail of clothes behind him as before and disappearing into the booth.)

COLIN. *(From the quick-change booth.)* Aw, shit!

CLARK. What's the matter?

COLIN. *(Coming out of the booth in his underwear, once again wearing the wig and bra.)* Where the hell are my shoes?

> *(He looks around a bit.)*

I must have left them in my dressing room.

> *(Beginning to pick up his clothes.)*

Aw, screw it. I'll do this later. Let's go work on your lines.

CLARK. *(As they begin to exit.)* Fine.

> *(Stopping.)*

Pussy Creek?

COLIN. Don't look at me.

> *(They exit.)*

PENELOPE. *(Offstage.)* Right this way, Congressman Bream.

BREAM. *(Offstage.)* Wow! This place looks so different.

PENELOPE. *(Offstage.)* Oh, yes, they did a wonderful job with the renovations, didn't they? And the acoustics are quite marvelous. Here, listen –

> *(She does a few voice exercises.)*

Mah! Mah! Pah! Pah! Booda dooba gooda dooga!

BREAM. *(Offstage.)* Uh, yes. Very impressive.

> *(The door upstage center opens and **BREAM** enters. He is clean-shaven, his hair neatly trimmed, and he's sporting a business suit. He looks every inch the president he hopes to become.)*

I hardly recognize it. You know, I won my first debate on this stage back when I was in the tenth grade.

> *(Looking around.)*

So what's the play you're doing?

PENELOPE. *(Following him in and leaving the door open.)* It's a new British farce. And your brother's playing the title role.

BREAM. *(Surprised.)* Roland is playing the lead? Say, is he around? I should say hello.

PENELOPE. Umm, yes, he's around. Somewhere.

> *(LORENA comes in from upstage right, checking out the backstage area. She's dressed in a conservative business suit and glasses.)*

LORENA. And this furniture on the stage?

PENELOPE. Oh, don't worry, we'll move all that out of the way and set up the podium and microphone for you.

LORENA. Excellent.

PENELOPE. And the sound and lights are at your disposal.

LORENA. What do you think, sir?

BREAM. Oh yes, yes it's great.

LORENA. *(To* **PENELOPE.***)* We're very sorry for the inconvenience to you and your theatre group.

PENELOPE. Oh, the Port Pilchard Players are only too happy to help. Anything for the Bream Team!

BREAM. Thank you, Ms. Witherspoon.

PENELOPE. Oh yes, we're all pulling for you – well most of us. Anyway, I know you have a lot to do, so I'll get out of your hair. If there's anything else you need, just come and find me. I'll be around. The speech is slated for three o'clock, is that right?

LORENA. That's right.

PENELOPE. *(Checking her watch.)* Gosh, that's in less than ninety minutes.

LORENA. Yes, and we've got a lot to do in that time. Congressman Bream has a photo shoot to get to.

PENELOPE. Well, I'll let you get on with it, then. I've got to make sure Roland went to get shorn.

> *(She exits through an upstage door.)*

BREAM. *(Turns to* **LORENA.***)* Well. We made it. After that incident at Pussy Creek, I never thought we'd get here on time.

LORENA. It's such an odd coincidence that poor man should collapse just as you were walking into the men's room.

BREAM. Oh it was no coincidence, Lorena.

(He pulls a small dart out of his pocket.)

LORENA. What is that?

BREAM. A tranquilizer dart. I retrieved it from his backside.

LORENA. Why would someone shoot some random guy with a tranquilizer dart?

BREAM. Oh, he wasn't the target. That dart was meant for me.

LORENA. For you?

BREAM. Of course. It's just another in a long line of dirty tricks from the Weever campaign.

LORENA. No!

BREAM. Of course it was them. We are talking about the same people who hacked my medical records, and tried to convince the country I was crazy.

LORENA. True...

BREAM. *(Holding up the dart.)* And when this didn't work, they set up the bomb scare at the town hall. I'm telling you, the Weevils will do anything to stop me from making this speech.

LORENA. With good reason. You're about to change the country – no, the world! If the public hears what you have to say, you will clinch this election.

BREAM. *When* they hear what I have to say, you mean.

LORENA. After everything that's happened today, I'm worried. I mean, what are they going to try next? The race is too close to call at this point. We need this speech to put us over the top.

BREAM. Relax. We'll be fine.

(He looks at the dart.)

I hope that fella in Pussy Creek is going to be OK.

LORENA. He was awake by the time the paramedics arrived, although he was acting very strangely.

(Demonstrating as she describes this.)

He was flapping his arms and thrusting his head and cooing like a pigeon. Coo! Coo!

BREAM. *(Examining the dart and showing it to her.)* No wonder. The idiots shot him with bird tranquilizer.

LORENA. Bird tranquilizer? Why would they use that? It makes no sense!

BREAM. And they call me crazy.

LORENA. Well the whole thing played very well with the press.

BREAM. Sure did. They ate it up.

(Sincerely.) Anyway, you did a great job today, navigating us through all the craziness.

(He pats her on her shoulder, awkwardly.)

I don't know what I'd do without you.

(There is a brief moment between them. **LORENA** *smiles, then checks her watch.)*

LORENA. Well for one thing, you'd be late for all your appointments. Come on, it's time for your photo shoot at the old power plant.

BREAM. You mean our new Perch-oil Ureafication plant.

LORENA. Dices bien. Wait until the people of this town find out what you're going to do for them. They're going to put up a statue of you in Pilchard Park.

*(***WHITING*** *enters through the upstage right door. He is a youngish investigative reporter dressed in jeans and a baseball cap.)*

WHITING. Excuse me, Congressman Bream?

BREAM. Yes?

WHITING. *(Holding out his hand.)* Jim Whiting. I'm a reporter.

LORENA. I'm sorry, Mr. Whiting, but the press conference isn't for an hour and a half.

WHITING. I know, but I was just wondering if –

LORENA. Unfortunately, we're on our way to another event. We'll be taking questions after the press conference.

(*She moves toward the upstage right door.*)

BREAM. (*Affably.*) Sorry, but she's the boss!

WHITING. (*Stepping in front of* **BREAM.***) Oh please, sir, I just need five minutes of your time. It would mean so much to me.

LORENA. (*Indignantly.*) Excuse us.

(*She tries to move past but* **WHITING** *dashes in front of her and stands in the open doorway, barring their way.*)

Buen Dios!

(*To* **BREAM.***) Come on.

(*She ushers him toward the door.* **WHITING** *steps upstage of the door, slams it shut, races over to the upstage center door.* **LORENA** *ushers* **BREAM** *toward the upstage center door and opens it.* **WHITING** *stands in the doorway, barring their way again.*)

WHITING. (*Pleasantly.*) Hello again.

(**LORENA** *growls in frustration, grabs* **BREAM** *and leads him toward the upstage left door again.* **WHITING** *steps upstage, slams the upstage center door, races back to the upstage left door and bars their way once more.*)

I can do this all day.

LORENA. Out of our way, please.

(**WHITING** *leans against the doorjamb.*)

(*Getting out her phone and dialing.*)

OK, that's it, I'm calling security.

WHITING. No, please, don't do that!

(*Dropping to his knees and wrapping his arms around* **BREAM***'s legs.*)

You've got to give me an interview, sir! If you don't, I'll never get the job!

BREAM. What job? I thought you said you were a reporter.

WHITING. I am – provisionally, at least. It's my first day. And if you don't talk to me, it's going to be my last. My editor said to me, "Go and get me an exclusive with Raymond Bream. You do that, you're a reporter. You don't, you're unemployed." Please. I don't want to spend the rest of my life living in my parents' basement!

BREAM. *(Impressed.)* OK, OK, get up. Well kid, I've got to give you points for perseverance. You're going to need that if you want to be a reporter. What paper are you working for?

WHITING. The RNR.

> (**BREAM** *and* **LORENA** *take to one another in horror.)*

BREAM. The *Red Neck Report*? Are you kidding? I wouldn't give those libelous bastards the time of day! Get the hell out of here or I'll call security myself!

WHITING. No, please, you don't understand!

BREAM. Oh I understand perfectly. Have you been following what the RNR has been tweeting about me Mr. Whiting? That they should "lock me up." That I'm dangerously psychotic, that my power plant is a delusion. I'll have you know that P.U. is the greatest scientific discovery since the internal combustion engine.

WHITING. But P.U.? Couldn't you come up with a better name?

BREAM. It's an acronym! P for... Alright, you want an exclusive? Here it is – despite what the Weever administration and the RNR have been telling the world, I am *not* certifiable and P.U., whatever you may think of the name, actually works.

WHITING. But the scientific community has discredited the research –

BREAM. The scientific community has been gagged by President Weever. You've been listening to a bunch of government propaganda. Did you hear what happened to Heilbutt Zingel, the scientist who discovered this process? They cut off his funding, closed down his laboratory and even tried to deport him!

WHITING. Why?

BREAM. Why else? To keep their friends in Big Oil happy. Fortunately, despite their efforts, Doctor Zingel managed to perfect the process, and this afternoon we're going to prove to the world that it works.

WHITING. How?

BREAM. We've brought a sample of P.U. with us. Doctor Zingel and I are going to pour it into a Subaru out front and take a few of your media buddies for a spin.

WHITING. A Subaru, eh? Like the one in Weever's commercial, the one with all the cats?

BREAM. Same color, same model. It even has the same license plate.

WHITING. I see. Well... That's quite a story.

BREAM. Yes it is. Only problem is, your paper will never print it.

WHITING. Why not?

BREAM. Because they're not interested in the truth. All they care about is their political agenda, and any inconvenient facts that get in the way of it are conveniently ignored.

WHITING. What if I promised to print whatever you say, verbatim?

BREAM. Nice try, kid, but your editors will never go for it.

WHITING. *(Getting out his phone and dialing.)* Let's find out, shall we? Hello, Mr. Pike? It's Jim Whiting. I have a question about our deal. If I get this exclusive with Congressman Bream, will you promise to print whatever he says to me? ...You will? Can you repeat that, please?

> *(Holds the phone to* **BREAM***'s ear briefly, then takes it back.)*

Thank you, sir... What's that? ...I see.

(Looking at his watch.)

OK, I think I can do that... Thank you Mr. Pike.

(Hanging up.)

So, do we have a deal?

LORENA. Congressman, the photographer is waiting.

BREAM. *(To* **LORENA.***)* I know, I know.

(To **WHITING.***)* Alright Mr. Whiting, we have a deal. Meet us back here in an hour.

WHITING. That doesn't leave me much time to write my story. Mr. Pike told me I had to file it before your press conference.

LORENA. It's the best we can do.

WHITING. Well, I guess I've got enough here to get started.

(He heads toward one of the upstage doors.)

I'll be back in an hour. Thank you sir. You won't regret this.

(He exits.)

LORENA. What are you thinking? This is a waste of time. You know who reads the *Red Neck Report*. They'll never vote for you.

BREAM. Yes, and why is that? Because the RNR is the only thing they read. They think I'm some tree-hugging looney tune who belongs in a rubber room. Now, thanks to Whiting, we have a chance to set them straight. All we need to do is win over a small percentage of their readership, and we can clinch this election.

MANDY. *(Offstage.)* What the hell have I done with my bloody script?

> *(***MANDY** *enters from stage right still sporting her turban and now wearing a sexy, low-cut, flowing robe.)*

Oh, sorry, I didn't...

(Recognizing **BREAM.***)*

MANDY. OH!! It's you!!!

> *(She races over to him and grabs his hand, which she proceeds to kiss, shake, and generally abuse.)*

This is such an honor. I've been wanting to meet you for ages.

BREAM. It's a pleasure to meet you too, Miss...

MANDY. Miss. Randall. Mandy Randall. That's my handle. But please – everyone calls me Mandy. Unless they know me really well and then they call me Randy Mandy.

> *(She giggles suggestively.)*

BREAM. Well it's very nice to meet you Miss Randy, Miss Mandall, Miss Randall. But I'm afraid we're in a bit of a –

MANDY. Could I get your autograph?

LORENA. Sir, we really have to go.

BREAM. I'm sorry Miss Randall, I don't have a pen.

MANDY. I just happen to have one right here.

> *(She whips a Sharpie out of her cleavage.)*

BREAM. But I don't have anything to write on.

MANDY. Oh yes you do.

> *(She pulls open her robe, exposing a generous portion of her left breast.)*

Just sign here. Right next to my heart.

BREAM. *(He glances at* **LORENA***.)* Ummm...

> *(***LORENA** *spots one of the programs and picks it up, handing it to* **BREAM***.)*

Here, why don't we use this?

MANDY. Good idea.

> *(Taking the program from him and showing him the spot.)*

You can sign my picture.

BREAM. (*Surprised, looking at the picture then back to her.*) This...is you?

MANDY. I know, the lighting makes me look a hundred.

> (**BREAM** *signs the program under the following.*)

Too bad you won't be able to see me in *The Vicar's Knickers.*

BREAM. I beg your pardon?

MANDY. (*Indicating the program.*) Our play. Penelope says we're so much funnier than they were in the West End.

BREAM. I'm sure you are.

> (*Handing her back the program.*)

Here you go!

MANDY. Thank you. Time for a selfie.

> (*She whips out her phone, aims it at* **BREAM,** *then plants a kiss on his cheek. His shock and embarrassment register on his face just as the shutter clicks.*)

This is going right on Facebook.

> (*She checks it out and is horrified at what she sees. One of her hands shoots up to the turban.*)

Oh shit!

> (*She hurries off.*)

BREAM. Wow.

LORENA. Now sir, we'd better get you to that photo shoot.

BREAM. Oh yes.

(*As she guides him off.*) Thanks, Lorena. Without you I'd be late for my own funeral.

> (*They exit through upstage left door as* **GILL** *and* **SHARKEY** *enter upstage right. They are wearing sunglasses and are dressed in straw hats and carrying placards in red, orange, and blue. One reads "Make the Bream Dream*

Come True," the other reads "I'm on the Bream Team.")

SHARKEY. *(Looking at his Bream Team regalia.)* I feel dirty wearing this stuff.

GILL. Don't complain. It got us in the building didn't it?

(Under the following, they divest themselves of their Bream Team regalia and put it out of sight.)

SHARKEY. Barely. I've never seen so many Secret Service guys in my life.

GILL. Anyway, we wouldn't need to be here at all if it wasn't for your spectacular screw-up in Pussy Creek.

SHARKEY. *My* screw-up? I wasn't the one who shot the wrong guy.

GILL. Well. You're the one who texted me that Bream was coming into the bathroom.

SHARKEY. He *was* coming into the bathroom!

GILL. Yeah, but you neglected to mention there was a guy coming in right ahead of him! Jeez! Three hours I sat in that damn stall breathing coffee and donut fumes and then I end up plugging some innocent bystander – thanks to you!

SHARKEY. Well, I'm not the one who left that tranquilizer dart behind.

GILL. How was I supposed to retrieve it? Bream came in about a second after the guy hit the floor!

SHARKEY. They can trace that back to us, you know. You probably left your fingerprints on it.

GILL. Don't worry about that. We've got bigger fish to fry.

(Pulling out his phone.)

The story's all over the news. That means the President knows we messed up. We've got to find Bream and get him under wraps before this phone rings.

(**GILL**'s *phone rings. His ringtone is a particularly ominous rendition of "Hail to the Chief."*)*

Oh shit.

(Answering phone.) Yes, President Weever... Oh, the Dunkin' Donuts in Pussy Creek?

(Lying through his teeth.)

Yeah, we had a bit of a hiccup, but we sorted it out... The bomb scare? Yeah, that was us. We needed a diversion so we could regroup... No worries, Bream's in the bag... Yes, we've got him.

SHARKEY. What the hell...?

GILL. *(Covering the phone.)* Shh!

(Into the phone.) Yes, we're umm...in Port Pilchard, in the parking lot at the Community Center... Bream? Oh don't worry about him, he won't be making any speeches today. He's right here in the trunk of our car, sleeping like a baby.

(**SHARKEY** *does a facepalm.*)

When folks tune in to the six o'clock news tonight, they won't be hearing anything about Bream and his crazy P.U. scheme. Instead they'll be watching you telling them how great the next four years are gonna be... Thank you, President Weever.

(He hangs up.)

SHARKEY. Are you nuts? What did you say that for? You just lied to the president!

GILL. That wasn't a lie. It was an alternative fact.

SHARKEY. I don't think Weever's gonna see it that way.

GILL. Look, it may not be a fact yet, but it will be once we get our hands on Bream.

---

*Licensees must only use orchestrations of "Hail to the Chief" that are in the public domain.

SHARKEY. I don't get what's so important about stopping him from making this speech. Weever has been telling people for months that P.U. doesn't work.

GILL. That's the problem. It does work.

SHARKEY. What?? But we checked out the research, our scientists discredited the whole thing!

GILL. That's what they told the press.

SHARKEY. You mean the whole "It Stinks" campaign – that's all fake?

GILL. Sharkey, you've got a lot to learn about politics.

SHARKEY. Are you telling me P.U. is for real?

GILL. Not only is it for real, but they've got it up and running. We just found out last night that they have a sample of the fuel and Bream is going to unveil it today. We have to stop this news from getting out – until Tuesday, at least.

SHARKEY. What happens after that?

GILL. Once Weever is voted back into office we can keep P.U. tied up in environmental assessments while we get that illegal immigrant Zingel kicked out of the country.

SHARKEY. Zingel's an illegal immigrant?

GILL. No, dummy. We just *say* he's an illegal immigrant.

SHARKEY. *(As the penny drops.)* Oh, I get it.

GILL. *(To himself.)* Why do they always stick me with the slow ones?

SHARKEY. So how are we going to get rid of Bream?

GILL. Same as we originally planned. Only this time we're going to shoot the right person.

SHARKEY. Yeah, but first we've got to find him – and get him alone.

GILL. And make sure there are no witnesses.

SHARKEY. *(Looking around at the back of the set, the costumes, etc.)* What do you suppose is going on here?

GILL. Looks like someone's putting on a play.

*(He finds the programs, picks one up, and leafs through it. As he does this, **SHARKEY** goes through the costumes on the racks, finds a colorful smoking jacket and scarf. He puts the jacket on.)*

"*The Vicar's Knickers*, by Crispian Postlethwaite and Roger Dickey-Dennis."

(Snorts.)

Where do they get these names? Like anybody would call their kid "Crispian." "Presented by the Port Pilchard Players." Hmm. Community theatre. Pfff.

*(He turns and sees **SHARKEY** in his theatrical attire.)*

What the hell are you doing?

SHARKEY. *(Adopting a very dramatic attitude and slipping the scarf around **GILL**'s neck.)* What's the matter darling, don't you like it?

*(**GILL**, still holding the program, is just about to tear the scarf off when **PENELOPE** enters through one of the doors of the set.)*

PENELOPE. Oh, hello.

(Slightly frosty.) Who are you?

GILL. Oh, I'm, um...

*(With a look to **SHARKEY**.)*

We...we are, uh...

SHARKEY. *(Taking the program from **GILL**.)* The playwrights.

(With a surreptitious look down at the program.)

Roger Dickey-Dennis

*(Offering his hand to **PENELOPE**.)*

How do you do? And this is –

(Another quick look down.)

SHARKEY. Crispian Postlethwaite.

GILL. *(Doing a slow burn as he takes to* **SHARKEY,** *then turning to* **PENELOPE** *with a pained smile.)* Delighted.

PENELOPE. *(Over the moon with delight.)* Oh my goodness! Crispian Postlethwaite and Roger Dickey-Dennis? You mean you've come all the way from England just to see our little production?

GILL & SHARKEY. *(Looking at each other.)* England?

GILL. *(With his best attempt at a posh English accent.)* Yes, that's right. Good old Blighty. What ho! Jolly hockey sticks.

PENELOPE. What?

GILL. And you are...?

PENELOPE. Oh, I'm sorry.

> *(Offering her hand.)*

Penelope Witherspoon. It's such an honor to meet you. I'm directing your wonderful play. By the way, I hope you don't mind, but we've made a few small improvements to some of the jokes. Particularly in the first act – it's a little slow off the top, don't you think?

GILL. *(Utterly at a loss.)* Well, that's – fine. Isn't it, Roger?

> **(SHARKEY,** *unaware that he's the one being addressed, doesn't respond.* **GILL** *nudges him.)*

Roger!

SHARKEY. *(Also with a posh English accent.)* Huh? Oh, yes, I suppose. Jolly good, what?

PENELOPE. This is so exciting! It's positively raining celebrities today. First Raymond Bream, and now you!

GILL. *(With a glance to* **SHARKEY.)** Raymond Bream? Here?

PENELOPE. Yes! He's our hometown hero and if the people of Port Pilchard have anything to say about it, he's going to be our next president.

GILL. You don't say?

PENELOPE. Oh yes. He's making a speech in a little while, right here on our set!

GILL. Oh really?

PENELOPE. Yes, he's having a press conference in just over an hour.

GILL. Oh, is he here? We'd be thrilled to meet him, wouldn't we, Roger?

SHARKEY. *(Deadpan.)* Delighted.

PENELOPE. Well he's gone off, actually. He had to go somewhere for a photo shoot. But he should be back any time now.

GILL. I see. Perhaps we'll wait, then.

> (**MOLLY** *comes in through one of the doors upstage, carrying a flower arrangement.*)

MOLLY. Oh Penelope, there you are. Any sign of Roland?

PENELOPE. No, not yet. Who are those for?

MOLLY. Mandy, of course. Listen, I was thinking we could use some of her flowers to spruce up the stage a little bit for the congressman's speech.

PENELOPE. That's a lovely idea!

MOLLY. *(Moving toward the dressing rooms.)* Right. I'll go and ask her.

PENELOPE. Molly, wait! I need to introduce you to someone first. Molly McQueen, meet Crispian Postlethwaite and Roger Dickey-Dennis – the authors of *The Vicar's Knickers*!

GILL. How do you do?

SHARKEY. Charmed.

MOLLY. *(Shaking hands.)* How lovely to meet you! What a nice surprise! Congratulations on your wedding, by the way.

GILL & SHARKEY. *(No accent.)* Wedding?

PENELOPE. Yes, we read all about it in *Hello Magazine*.

> (**GILL** *and* **SHARKEY** *take to one another. Slowly,* **GILL** *reaches over and takes* **SHARKEY***'s hand.*)

SHARKEY. Yes, we're so thrilled we could finally make it legal.

(Swinging GILL's arm back and forth and batting his eyes at him.)

SHARKEY. Aren't we, Roger?

GILL. *(Reluctantly.)* Ecstatic... Crispy.

MOLLY. *(Looking down at their hands.)* Could I see your rings?

GILL. *(With a look to SHARKEY.)* Rings?

SHARKEY. Oh, rings are so passé. We decided to go with tattoos instead.

(GILL looks at him.)

PENELOPE. Tattoos?

SHARKEY. *(Flirtatiously.)* Yes, but we can't possibly show you where.

(He turns to PENELOPE and MOLLY. GILL is horror-struck. An awkward beat.)

MOLLY. Well, I'd better deliver these flowers.

(She exits to the dressing rooms.)

PENELOPE. Yes, I should get going as well. I've got a trillion things to do. Oh, that reminds me –

(Handing them each a lanyard and ID card.)

You're going to need these to get in and out of the building. It's like Fort Knox around here! Now please make yourselves at home.

(Pointing offstage right.)

There's food and drinks in the kitchen, if you're hungry. I'd better go and make sure front of house has somewhere to put you. We're totally sold out, you know! What a wonderful surprise, having you two here! I can't wait to tell the cast!

(She exits through one of the doors upstage.)

GILL. Thanks a lot, "Mrs. Postlethwaite." You just had to put that stupid outfit on, didn't you? Now we're stuck pretending to be a couple of gay Limeys for the rest of the afternoon.

SHARKEY. Well, look at the bright side. I've just given us the perfect cover. At least now we're free to hang around until Bream gets back.

> (**ROLAND** *enters upstage center, still sporting his long hair and beard and carrying a pint bottle in a brown paper bag.*)

ROLAND. Hey – who are you?

SHARKEY. Oh hello. We're the playwrights.

> (*Stepping in and offering his hand.*)

Crispian Musselwhite. And this is, uh, Roger Dickey... something.

ROLAND. How's it goin', eh?

> (*Takes a swig from the bottle in the brown paper bag, then looks at* **GILL** *and* **SHARKEY** *and offers it to them.*)

Scotch?

SHARKEY. No, we're English, actually.

ROLAND. Huh? Listen –

> (*Indicating the bottle.*)

Let's keep this between us, right?

> (*He puts a finger to his lips as he crosses to the props table, pulls out a boot from underneath, and secretes the bottle inside.*)

Now, what was I supposed to be doing?

(*Calling as he exits upstage center.*) Penelope!

> (**SHARKEY** *and* **GILL** *take to one another.*)

GILL. I guess that was the vicar.

SHARKEY. (*Holding up a large pair of ugly undies he's found on one of the costume racks.*) And these must be the knickers.

GILL. What the hell kind of a play is this? No wonder the president wants to cut funding to the arts.

> (MANDY *enters from the dressing rooms downstage right. She has shed her turban and her hair is down.*)

MANDY. Oh, there you are! Now, let me guess –

> (*Crossing to* GILL.)

You're Mr. Postlethwaite, and...

> (*Crossing to* SHARKEY.)

...You're Mr. Dickey-Dennis. Am I right?

SHARKEY. (*Unable to remember who is whom.*) Um...

GILL. (*Putting on the British accent.*) Whatever you say.

MANDY. Molly didn't tell me you were both so handsome.

GILL. (*Flattered.*) Oh, thank you.

MANDY. It's so nice to meet you. I'm Mandy Randall. That's my handle. But please, call me Randy. I mean Mandy.

GILL. (*His eyes fixated on her cleavage, momentarily forgetting his accent.*) I kind of preferred the first one.

MANDY. (*Giggling as she rearranges her bosom.*) Well, I answer to both! Now, gentlemen, I hate to impose, but if you've got a moment, I'd love to pick your brains about my big speech in Act Two.

GILL. (*Beat.*) Uh, we'd love to help, but I'm afraid we've got to go to the, uh...uh...

SHARKEY. Loo!

GILL. Yes.

> (*Beat.*)

It was a very long flight.

MANDY. The loo – together?

SHARKEY. Oh yes. We do everything together.

> (*Taking* GILL's *hand.*)

Don't we, Crispy?

MANDY. (*Flirtatiously.*) Well, if you have some time later, come visit. I'd love to get to know you better.

(Crossing downstage right.)

I'll be in my dressing room. Just down here on the right.

(She stops in the doorway and turns back to them.)

What a waste. All the cute ones are either married or gay. Or both.

(She exits downstage right. **GILL** *admires her retreating figure and gives a low whistle of appreciation.)*

GILL. Gee, maybe there *is* something to pursuing the arts.

SHARKEY. Don't you mean arse?

GILL. Can I help it if women find me irresistible? Anyway, we need to get moving here. Get on the horn and book us a motel room.

SHARKEY. Aren't you taking this gay playwright thing a bit too far?

GILL. It's not for us, stupid. It's for Bream.

SHARKEY. *(Getting out his phone.)* Oh, right.

GILL. Now while you're doing that, let's go to the car and get that tranquilizer gun.

(They exit through the doors upstage right just as **ROLAND** *enters upstage left from the stage.)*

(He crosses to retrieve his bottle. He picks it up and goes to take a swig.)

PENELOPE. *(Offstage, from the front of house area.)* Roland!

*(***ROLAND** *quickly dashes into the quick-change booth with the bottle.* **MOLLY** *enters from downstage right, wheeling in a small podium with a microphone attached. She looks around.)*

MOLLY. *(Calling out to her.)* He's not back here, Pen.

(She wheels the podium through one of the doors to the set and onto the stage. As soon

as she exits the backstage area, **ROLAND** *reappears from the quick-change booth, bottle in hand, and takes a sip.)*

PENELOPE. *(Offstage.)* Oh my lord, that man is going to be the death of me.

(Her voice fading as she exits the auditorium.)

We've got to get him to the barber shop. We can't have our vicar being played by a sasquatch.

*(***ROLAND*** quickly replaces the bottle in the boot and exits onto the stage through the door upstage left as ***MOLLY*** comes backstage from upstage right to get a cable.)*

ROLAND. *(From the stage.)* Somebody looking for me?

MOLLY. Where have you been?

ROLAND. *(Entering upstage left.)* Right here.

MOLLY. We've got to get you to the barber.

ROLAND. *(Hopefully.)* You've got to get me to the bar?
(Off **MOLLY***'s look.)* Oh yeah – the barber – that's what I was supposed to be doing.

(He starts to exit.)

MOLLY. Stop!!

ROLAND. What's wrong?

MOLLY. You can't go like that.

ROLAND. Like what?

MOLLY. The costume.

ROLAND. What?

(Looking at himself.)

Oh, right.

(Under the following, **ROLAND** *takes off his cassock with attached clerical collar, tossing them on the floor. He then puts on a suit jacket [matching the pants he's wearing] hanging on the back of one of the chairs.* **COLIN** *enters*

*from the dressing room area downstage right
with an armload of his costume.)*

MOLLY. What are you up to, Colin?

COLIN. Thought I'd work on my quick-change.

(He starts to cross to the quick-change booth.)

MOLLY. That can wait. I need someone to take Roland to
the barber.

COLIN. What?

ROLAND. No you don't. I can manage perfectly well on my
own.

MOLLY. No, you can't. You need supervision.

ROLAND. You don't trust me?

MOLLY. Not for a second. Colin's taking you and that's that.
Shave and a haircut.

ROLAND. Two bits.

*(He cracks himself up. **MOLLY** pulls a
microphone cable out of a box under the
props table.)*

COLIN. Can't you get somebody else?

MOLLY. Look, I'd do it myself, but I'm up to my eyeballs
here.

(She takes the cable out onto the stage.)

COLIN. OK, OK, come on, Rasputin.

*(**ROLAND** and **COLIN** exit through the door
upstage right onto the stage as **MANDY** enters
from the dressing rooms carrying two flower
arrangements. She sets them on the props
table and fusses with them.)*

MOLLY. *(Offstage.)* Pen, are you out there?

PENELOPE. *(On the Tannoy.)* Yes, I'm in the booth, darling.

MOLLY. *(Offstage.)* Can you do me a favor and switch on the
sound?

PENELOPE. *(On Tannoy.)* Of course. Now, which of these
buttons is it? Oh yes – here we are.

(Suddenly the lights go out.)

MANDY. Hey!

PENELOPE. *(On Tannoy.) Sorry! Just a second...*

> *(A beat, then the lights come back on. **MANDY** finds herself face to face with **CLARK**, who has entered in the blackout. His shirt is covered in green goo, which is also splashed all over his face. They both scream.)*

MANDY. What happened to you?

PENELOPE. *(On Tannoy.) It must be this one –*

> *(We hear a huge wave of feedback.)*

Sorry! I'm not very good with technology.

MOLLY. *(Offstage.) Could you turn it down a bit, please?*

> *(The feedback disappears.)*

CLARK. Judy and I were making guacamole and the blender exploded.

MANDY. Oh. That's lucky!

> *(They both giggle. **CLARK** crosses to the costume racks and begins riffling through them.)*

MOLLY. *(Offstage, on microphone.) I just want to check the levels, Pen. How does this sound? One, two, one, two...*

> *(**CLARK** selects the only option he can find – a frilly woman's blouse – from the costume racks and crosses toward the dressing rooms.)*

MANDY. What are you doing?

CLARK. *(Pulling at his shirt.)* I need something to wear while this is in the wash.

> *(**MANDY** cracks up at the sight of him.)*

What's so funny?

MANDY. You look like a Jackson Pollock painting.

CLARK. You think I look bad, you should see Judy.

JUDY. *(Offstage, from the dressing rooms.)* Clark! I need you!

CLARK. Coming Judy.

> *(He exits.)*

PENELOPE. *(Offstage, still on the Tannoy.) Do you need anything else, Molly? I've got to dash.*

MOLLY. *(Offstage, still on microphone.) No, that's fine, thanks.*

PENELOPE. *(On Tannoy.) Right, then.*

MANDY. *(Admiring her work with the flowers.)* There. Much better.

> *(Calling to* **MOLLY**.*)* Where would you like these flowers, Molly?

MOLLY. *(Offstage, on microphone.) Just leave them back there for now. I'll come get them when I'm finished with this. Oh, Congressman. We're just setting up your microphone.*

> *(As soon as she hears Bream's name,* **MANDY** *adjusts her bosom and hair, then rushes into the quick-change booth to check herself in the mirror.)*

BREAM. *(Offstage.)* That's great. I was hoping to get a chance to run through my speech.

MOLLY. *(Offstage, on microphone.) Sure, whatever you like.*

> *(***BREAM** *enters through one of the doors upstage center, followed by* **LORENA**.*)*

BREAM. That went well.

LORENA. Yes, and much quicker than expected.

> *(***LORENA**'*s phone buzzes as she gets a text. She reads it.)*

Oh, excellent! The fuel's arrived! I'd better go check it out. Have you got your speech?

BREAM. *(Pulling his phone out of his pants pocket.)* Right here on my phone.

LORENA. Good. Text me if you need me.

> *(She exits through one of the doors upstage center. Once she leaves,* **BREAM** *heaves a big*

sigh of relief. It's the first moment he's had to himself all day. He takes off his jacket and hangs it on the back of one of the chairs. He sits down on the chair, winces, and does a few head rolls to alleviate a stiff neck. Meanwhile, **MANDY** *comes out of the quick-change booth and slinks up behind him.)*

BREAM. God, what I wouldn't give for a massage.

> **(MANDY** *immediately obliges by putting her hands on his shoulders. He jumps in surprise and turns to see who it is.)*

MANDY. Relax. It's just me, Mandy.

> *(She begins kneading his shoulders with her fingers.)*

BREAM. *(Groaning with pleasure.)* Oh...ohhhhhhh...

MANDY. *(Leaning forward and whispering in his ear.)* I'm also known as "Handy Mandy."

BREAM. Oh God!

MANDY. *(Continuing to massage him.)* Ooh, feel those muscles. They're like rocks! You poor dear.

> **(BREAM** *grunts in appreciation, melting now, unable to form a sentence.)*

Of course, this campaign must be so stressful for you...

BREAM. You've said a mouthful there.

MANDY. You need to find a way to relax. What do you do for fun?

BREAM. I play squash.

MANDY. Squash? I know a game that's much more fun and you can play it anywhere. It's called "squish".

> *(At this, she leans forward and sandwiches his head between her boobs. He snaps out of his trance and extricates himself.)*

BREAM. Uh, thanks for the offer, Randy – uh, Handy – uh, Mandy. But I really have to get back to work.

MANDY. You know what they say about all work and no play...

BREAM. I know, but this really isn't the time. I have to run through my speech.

MANDY. *(With innuendo.)* Is it very long?

BREAM. Uh. Not really. Average. Three minutes or so.

MANDY. Excellent. I'll be back in four.

(She slinks off downstage right to the dressing rooms.)

BREAM. Oh, God.

(Shakes off the Mandy moment.)

Right. Back to work.

(He turns front, pacing, looking at his phone, and begins to rehearse.)

Ladies and gentlemen...

(Clearing his throat and lowering his voice.)

Ladies and gentlemen, members of the press, and citizens of the greatest town in the country, my home town of Port Pilchard...

*(The upstage right door opens and **GILL** and **SHARKEY** creep through it. They check to make sure the coast is clear. **GILL** aims his tranquilizer gun at **BREAM**.)*

I want to thank you all for coming here today...

*(He shoots a dart at **BREAM**. It hits him in the rear and he drops like a stone.)*

SHARKEY. Wow! Those things work fast.

GILL. Gimme a hand. We've got to get him out of sight.

*(They cross in and pick up **BREAM**, sitting him on a nearby chair. He slumps over.)*

SHARKEY. Now what?

GILL. We're gonna take him to the motel to sleep it off.

SHARKEY. What if somebody recognizes him?

GILL. Good point.

> *(He looks around and spots Roland's discarded cassock.)*

Here. This'll work perfectly.

> *(**GILL** sits **BREAM** up and they struggle to put him into the cassock, attaching it with the Velcro fastening down the back.)*

SHARKEY. *(Having difficulty dressing him.)* Phew! This isn't easy is it?

GILL. *(Standing back to look.)* He's still too recognizable.

SHARKEY. Hold on.

> *(He looks at the props table and picks up a cheesy-looking beard and hat.)*

> *(Crossing back.)*

Here. Let's try this.

> *(He puts the beard over **BREAM**'s ears and shoves the hat on his head.)*

What do you think?

GILL. It's a bit Hasidic, but it'll do.

SHARKEY. Wait a second. Once they've discovered Bream is missing, they're going to put out an All Points Bulletin on him. How are we going to get away?

GILL. Don't worry. I've got it covered.

> *(Picking up Bream's phone from the floor.)*

This is Bream's phone. I'm just going to record a little text and send it to that Spanish terrier of his.

SHARKEY. Well, talk slowly for heaven's sake. That thing has a hard time understanding you.

GILL. *(Dictating into the phone.)* "Can't take this anymore. Period. Need some time off. Checking in to the loony bin. All caps. NO MORE MESSAGES, semicolon. They're taking my phone."

> *(Clicks it off.)*

There. Now when people find out he's missing, they'll just assume he's had a nervous breakdown.

SHARKEY. That should work. Weever's been warning people about that for months.

(**GILL** *puts Bream's phone in his pocket.*)

Wait a minute. We can't take that with us.

GILL. *(Pulling the phone out again.)* Why not?

SHARKEY. They'll track us. GPS.

GILL. Good thinking.

(*He tosses the phone aside.*)

Now go and bring the car around and let's get going.

SHARKEY. OK.

(*He heads for the upstage left door.*)

GILL. I'll get the rabbi here out of sight till you get back. Oh and remember – if anybody asks, you're Roger Dickey Dumplings the British playwright.

SHARKEY. *(Affecting English accent.)* Oh, yes, Darling.

(*He exits, closing the door.*)

GILL. Phew.

(*He mops his face with a hanky. Still in need of stress relief, he remembers Roland's boot. He crosses to the table, picks up the boot, and pulls out the bottle.*)

(*He opens it, drains it, and puts it back in the boot. He then crosses to the quick-change booth and checks it out.*)

This'll do.

(*He crosses back to* **BREAM**. *With a great deal of effort he hauls* **BREAM** *to his feet, turns him around in front of himself like a giant puppet, and walks him toward the quick-change booth. He stops at the props table upstage center for a breather and* **BREAM** *collapses face-first onto the table.* **GILL** *tries to break his fall and ends up collapsing face-first onto* **BREAM,** *his arm trapped under him. He struggles to release it. At this moment* **MANDY** *enters downstage right.)*

GILL. I didn't realize how hard this was going to be.

MANDY. Bet I could make it harder.

GILL. *(Jumping out of his skin.)* AAAAGH!
   (Desperately.) This isn't what it looks like.

MANDY. Don't worry, I'm very broad-minded.

GILL. *(English accent.)* No, no, no. You don't understand –

   (He turns to her, letting go of **BREAM,** *who slips to his knees.* **GILL** *grabs him around the waist.)*

He's…three sheets to the wind.

MANDY. Oh, no! Don't tell me he's fallen off the wagon?

   (With a look to **GILL** *still hunched over* **BREAM.**)

And fallen from grace too, by the look of it. My goodness, what would Roger say if he saw you?

GILL. Who? Oh, Roger. Oh don't mind him. He's…very broad-minded too.

MANDY. Well, that's not true of everyone around here, "Crispy." You need to be discreet about this sort of thing. Why don't you two use my dressing room? I've got a very comfy chaise lounge in there.

GILL. Thank you, er –

MANDY. Mandy.

GILL. Mandy.

MANDY. *(She starts out and then turns back.)* Oh. Just give me a minute. Young Percy is sleeping like a baby in there, dear boy.

   (She exits to the dressing room, swinging her hips. **GILL** *watches her go.)*

GILL. And I thought politicians were easy.

(**SHARKEY** *bolts in from upstage left.*)

SHARKEY. I got good news and bad news. The good news is, the car's in the alley with the engine running and the trunk wide open.

GILL. And the bad news?

SHARKEY. The Secret Service are doing a sweep of the entire building. We've got to get out of here now.

GILL. Right.

(*Together they haul* **BREAM** *up.*)

MALE VOICE. (*Offstage.*) *We'll need to check the backstage area now, Ma'am.*

(**SHARKEY** *and* **GILL** *look at each other in panic.*)

SHARKEY. Oh no!

GILL. Quick!

(*He indicates the downstage left emergency door. They begin to lug* **BREAM** *toward it.*)

MOLLY. (*Offstage.*) No problem. Follow me.

(**MOLLY** *opens the upstage right door.*)

(*Gesturing offstage, to the agent.*) This way...

(*As she enters,* **GILL** *and* **SHARKEY** *push open the crash bar. A loud alarm goes off. Unseen by* **MOLLY**, *they haul* **BREAM** *out the door as* **MOLLY** *reacts to the alarm.*)

(*Blackout.*)

End of Act One

ACT TWO

(A few moments later. The stage is empty.)

ROLAND. *(Offstage.)* Hello? HELLOO? Where is everybody?

> *(**ROLAND** enters from upstage center. He is shorn and shaved and looks exactly like his brother. Somewhat baffled, he shrugs, crosses to the props table, and picks up the boot. He pulls the bottle out, sees that it's empty.)*

Damn. Oh well. There's more where that came from.

> *(He exits upstage left as **JUDY**, **CLARK**, **COLIN**, and **MANDY** enter downstage left through the emergency door. **CLARK** is now cleaned up and clad in the frilly shirt he took from the costume rack earlier. **JUDY** wears an apron over a sweatsuit.)*

COLIN. First a bomb scare, then a fire alarm. What's next, a drone strike?

JUDY. *(Pointing at **CLARK**'s frilly shirt.)* You realize you're wearing my costume, Clark.

CLARK. I'm quite aware of that, thank you. I'm lucky I made it back in here with my honor intact; I was being seriously cruised by that Secret Service guy.

MANDY. Did anyone see Roger and Crispy out there?

CLARK. Who?

MANDY. The playwrights. They were right here just before the alarm went off.

CLARK. Maybe they're the ones who set it off. They probably didn't realize that door had an alarm on it.

JUDY. *(Pointing to the big sign on the door.)* Oh, so they can write but they can't read?

MANDY. Maybe they were trying to help him walk it off.

JUDY. Help who walk what off?

MANDY. Well, Roland was just here with Crispy, and he was so drunk he couldn't stand up.

JUDY. Oh, no!

CLARK. *(Overlapping.)* Not again...

JUDY. I told you it was only a matter of time.

COLIN. What? Roland's not drunk. I just brought him back from the barber's. I stopped off at the box office to check on tickets for tonight, and he was just ahead of me, coming into the auditorium when the fire alarm went off.

MANDY. But I just saw him back here with Crispy. He was completely out of it. Ooh, just a minute. I forgot all about young Percy.

(She races out downstage right.)

(Calling as she goes.) Percy? Wake up, darling!

CLARK. How could anybody have slept through that alarm?

COLIN. After a session with Mandy, he's lucky he's still breathing.

JUDY. *(Archly.)* You ought to know.

COLIN. *(With a look to* **JUDY**.*)* Anyway, I don't know what she's talking about. Roland is fine – well, for Roland. You should see him, though. Now that he's all cleaned up, he's a dead ringer for his brother.

CLARK. Well they are twins.

COLIN. Yeah, but he's the absolute spitting image of Raymond. He almost looks like he could be running for office!

JUDY. God forbid.

CLARK. Let's not start that again. Come on, Judy, we better finish cleaning up that kitchen. It looks like Kermit the Frog blew himself up in there.

JUDY. Damn blender.

(She and **CLARK** *exit downstage right.)*

COLIN. *(To **CLARK** as he exits.)* When are we going to work on that stupid quick-change?

> *(**LORENA** enters from upstage center, very distraught.)*

LORENA. Congressman? Are you back here?

> *(Seeing **COLIN** coming out of the quick-change booth with an armful of his costume pieces.)*

Have you seen señor Bream?

COLIN. Nope. Sorry. There's still a big crowd out in the parking lot. Maybe he hasn't made it back into the building yet. He could be in the kitchen, I suppose. Let me have a look for you.

LORENA. That's very kind of you. Thank you.

COLIN. *(To himself, with a sigh, as he exits downstage right.)* Ah, to hell with it. I'll do the quick-change in my dressing room.

> *(He exits as **PENELOPE** enters upstage center.)*

LORENA. Oh, Penelope. There you are. Have you seen the congressman?

PENELOPE. No. Why?

LORENA. I just got the most disturbing text from him. Look –

> *(She hands **PENELOPE** her phone. **PENELOPE** reads.)*

PENELOPE. "Can't fake tits Sandy. More periods. Need sunshine. Cough. Protecting the boonies Ben. Al Capp KNOWS MORE MASSAGES. Sammy's colon's tickling my bone." What the hell does that mean?

LORENA. Stupid phone. Luckily I speak fluent text.

> *(Taking the phone and reading the correct version.)*

"Can't take this anymore, period. Need some time off, semicolon. Checking in to the loony bin. All caps – no more messages, semicolon. They're taking my phone."

PENELOPE. What??

LORENA. I don't understand. "Can't take this anymore"? It makes no sense. He lives for this campaign. He's on the verge of winning the election. He'd never quit now.

PENELOPE. Have you tried calling him?

LORENA. About a dozen times. I'll try again.

> (*She presses a button and we hear Bream's cell phone ringing. It's a very upbeat instrumental version of "The Star-Spangled Banner."** LORENA looks around, spots the phone, crosses to it, and picks it up.*)

What's his phone doing here? He never goes anywhere without it. There's something very fishy about all this...

PENELOPE. What do you think has happened?

LORENA. Well, let's see... First we announce that he's making a big policy speech this afternoon at the town hall, and someone calls in a bomb threat. So we change venues and then Mr. Bream inexplicably disappears, leaving behind a bizarre text and the phone that he is never, ever without.

> (*Looks up at* PENELOPE.)

I think he's been abducted.

PENELOPE. Abducted? But who would do that?

LORENA. Who else? Weever.

PENELOPE. Weever?

LORENA. Well they've been claiming for months that he's crazy and now, just before making the biggest speech of his career – he suddenly checks himself into a psychiatric facility? Doesn't that sound a bit convenient to you?

PENELOPE. I can't believe that.

LORENA. Believe it. They tried to shoot him in Pussy Creek.

---

*Licensees must only use orchestrations of "The Star-Spangled Banner" that are in the public domain.

PENELOPE. *(Alarmed.)* Shoot him *where?*

LORENA. In Pussy Creek, in the bathroom with a tranquilizer dart.

PENELOPE. Sounds like a game of "Clue."

LORENA. I think they intended to grab him there, but they shot the wrong guy.

PENELOPE. Heavens to Betsy! Well what are we waiting for? Let's tell the Secret Service.

LORENA. We can't do that.

PENELOPE. Why not?

LORENA. If they're involved, the media will get wind of it. All they have to do is hear the words "psychiatric facility" and that'll be the end of our campaign. I have to find him myself. *(Checking her watch.)* Mierda. It's 2:30. Text me if you see him!

> *(She exits through the door upstage left just as* **WHITING** *enters from upstage right. He crosses to* **PENELOPE.**)*

WHITING. Hello.

PENELOPE. Oh, hello. Who are you?

WHITING. Jim Whiting from the RNR.

PENELOPE. RNR?

WHITING. The *Red Neck Report.* I'm here for my interview with Congressman Bream. Do you know where he is?

PENELOPE. *(A hand rising to her heart, under her breath.)* Good question.

WHITING. I beg your pardon?

PENELOPE. *(Tapping her chest.)* I said, "Indigestion." He's been committed – I mean, he had a prior commitment.

WHITING. Yes, I know. The photo shoot.

PENELOPE. Yes, that's it! I'm afraid he's not back yet.

WHITING. That's OK. I'm a little early.

PENELOPE. I see. Well, why don't you make yourself comfortable in the kitchen? You can help yourself to some snacks if you like – although I'd steer clear of the guacamole if I were you. We're having our opening night party tonight.

WHITING. Opening night?

PENELOPE. Yes!

(Hustling him toward the downstage right exit.)

Perhaps you could stay and see the show. It's going to be a very special evening. The playwrights are here – all the way from England!

*(And he's off. **PENELOPE** collects herself for a moment. Suddenly the emergency door opens and **BREAM** staggers in, still dressed in the vicar's cassock and hat but now without the beard, rubbing his sore behind. He's still recovering from the effects of the tranquilizer. One of these is a spasm in his neck muscles which causes him to periodically thrust his head forward like a pigeon. This is accompanied by a cooing sound. He's very disoriented. Seeing his cassock, hat, and disheveled state, **PENELOPE** assumes this is **ROLAND**.)*

Oh my goodness – is that you?

BREAM. *(Slightly slurring his words.)* I...think so.

PENELOPE. It's amazing. You look exactly like your brother.

BREAM. Yes, people always say that.

(He thrusts his head and coos like a pigeon.)

PENELOPE. Good lord, what's happened to you?

BREAM. I have no idea. One minute I was rehearsing my speech, and the next thing I knew I woke up in some motel room.

PENELOPE. Oh dear. Not again.

(He weaves unsteadily toward upstage center.)

Where are you going now?

BREAM. I need to rehearse.

PENELOPE. *(Bringing him back.)* No dear, not just now. I don't think that's a very good idea. Tell you what – why don't you go and sleep it off?

> *(She begins to usher him toward the dressing rooms, then has a change of heart.)*

On second thought, you'd better get out of that costume before you throw up on it.

> *(She wheels him around toward the quick-change booth. He resists, flapping his arms, thrusting his head, and cooing all the while.)*

Oh heavens. I think this is the worst I've ever seen you.

> *(LORENA enters, sees BREAM, and is immensely relieved.)*

LORENA. Gracias a Dios! There you are!

> *(BREAM looks behind himself.)*

But what are you doing in those clothes?

BREAM. *(Looking down.)* Oh my God.

> *(Looks up at her, distraught.)*

Why am I wearing a dress?

PENELOPE. This isn't who you think it is. This is his brother.

LORENA. *(To PENELOPE, amazed.)* Oh, Dios mio. They're identical.

> *(He thrusts his head and coos a couple of times. LORENA looks to PENELOPE in confusion. PENELOPE mimes a drinking motion behind BREAM's back. LORENA nods in understanding.)*

BREAM. I don't feel very well. I need to lie down.

> *(He crosses into the quick-change booth.)*

PENELOPE. Good idea.

(Confidentially.) He's a lot to put up with, but he's worth it. Very good actor, you know.

(Calling to him.) And take that costume off!

> *(WHITING enters from downstage right.)*

WHITING. Time to start the interview. Where's our candidate?

LORENA. He's – a little tied up at the moment.

WHITING. Hey, we had a deal, remember? If I'm going to get my scoop, I'm going to need some time to file the story.

LORENA. Just give us a few minutes.

> (**WHITING** *exits downstage right.*)
>
> (*Gesturing toward the downstage right exit.*)

He can't find out Congressman Bream is missing. We have to keep Whiting occupied until he comes back.

PENELOPE. Oh that's no problem. I know how to buy us some time.

LORENA. How?

PENELOPE. In a word, Mandy.

LORENA. Mandy? What can she do?

PENELOPE. You name it.

LORENA. Well, can she keep him busy for, say, half an hour?

PENELOPE. She can keep him busy all afternoon if necessary. And then there's the recovery time.

(*Calling.*) Oh, Mandy…

> (*As* **PENELOPE** *exits downstage right,* **LORENA** *discovers Bream's jacket on the back of a chair. She picks it up.*)

LORENA. Oh!

> (*Her phone rings.*)

(*Answering.*) Si, hola… No, no sign of him. Have you found anything? ¿Que? A beard? …Alright, never mind, I'm on my way.

> (*She pockets her phone and exits downstage left through the emergency door, carrying the jacket.* **BREAM** *emerges from the quick-change booth and wanders off through the upstage left door. As the door closes,* **GILL** *and* **SHARKEY** *enter upstage right.*)

SHARKEY. Where the hell is he?

GILL. He's got to be here somewhere, he's making his big announcement any minute. Shit, how did he wake up so fast?

SHARKEY. Well, don't look at me. You're the one who sent me out for pizza. You're the one who left him alone.

GILL. I didn't leave him alone. I was right there in the bathroom. I even left the door open!

SHARKEY. Fat lot of good that did.

GILL. Didn't you say that stuff was supposed to keep him out for at least eight hours?

SHARKEY. That's what the directions said.

GILL. What's it called again?

SHARKEY. *(Pulling a small package from his suit pocket and reading the label.)* "AH-VEE-AN."

GILL. What? Let me see that.

> *(He takes the package from* **SHARKEY** *and reads it himself.)*

That's not "AH-VEE-AN," you idiot, it's "avian." This is bird tranquilizer!

SHARKEY. Bird tranquilizer? No wonder he woke up so quick.

> *(***GILL** *smacks him. His phone rings with its "Hail to the Chief" ringtone.)**

GILL. *(Answering.)* Yes, President Weever. Oh yes, Bream's out like a light... I think the less you know about the details, the better. Plausible deniability and all that... Yes, don't worry. He's not going anywhere... That's right, we can proceed as planned... Thank you, President Weever.

> *(He hangs up.)*

SHARKEY. *(Who has been tearing his hair out throughout this conversation.)* What the hell did you say that for?

---

*Licensees must only use orchestrations of "Hail to the Chief" that are in the public domain.

GILL. Relax, we'll be fine. All we have to do is grab Bream again.

SHARKEY. But how do we find him?

(Points to the upstage center door.)

It's not like he's going to walk through that door all by himself.

*(**ROLAND** walks through the door all by himself. He's carrying another brown paper bag with a bottle in it. He sees **GILL** and **SHARKEY** and smiles companionably.)*

ROLAND. How's it goin', fellas?

(He crosses to the props table, pulls another pint bottle of whiskey out of the bag, and has a long shot.)

SHARKEY. *(To **GILL**, sotto.)* What's up with him?

GILL. *(Sotto.)* He seems awful nonchalant for a guy who just got kidnapped.

ROLAND. *(Seeing them.)* Oh. Sorry.

(Proffering the bottle.)

Scotch? Oh no, English, I forgot.

*(He takes another slug. **GILL** and **SHARKEY** watch in amazement.)*

SHARKEY. *(Sotto.)* Holy crap! He's a lush.

GILL. *(Sotto.)* The Bream Team really kept that under wraps, didn't they? Quick – hit him with a few more darts.

*(**ROLAND** bends over to put the bottle in the boot as **SHARKEY** takes aim. **PENELOPE** enters from the dressing room. **SHARKEY** hides the gun behind his back.)*

PENELOPE. *(Seeing **ROLAND** in his suit and assuming he's **BREAM**.)* Oh, you're here!

ROLAND. Where else would I be?

PENELOPE. Thank God! I must let Lorena know. Have you all met?

(To **ROLAND.**) Allow me to introduce you to –

(To **GILL** *and* **SHARKEY.**) Mr. Postlethwaite and Mr. Dickey-Dennis.

> *(***GILL** *and* **SHARKEY** *affect their British personae.)*

GILL. Charmed.

SHARKEY. Delighted.

ROLAND. How's it goin'?

> *(***GILL**'s *phone rings with its "Hail to the Chief" ringtone.** **GILL** *and* **SHARKEY** *freeze and take to one another.)*

PENELOPE. What an unusual ring tone.

GILL. Yes, we just downloaded it.

SHARKEY. In honor of our visit. Excuse us.

> *(They bolt out the upstage left door.)*

PENELOPE. Lorena's absolutely beside herself. She's been looking for you everywhere!

ROLAND. Lorena eh? Mmmm. Sounds Spanish. Arriba! Arriba!

PENELOPE. Sorry? Anyway, where did you run off to?

ROLAND. You sent me to the barber shop, remember?

PENELOPE. The barber shop? Wait a minute –

> *(She looks him over closely. The penny drops.)*

Oh my heavens. Roland.

ROLAND. Don't tell me – I look SO much like my brother, right?

PENELOPE. No. You look *exactly* like him.

> *(Looking him over closely.)*

My goodness, it's creepy.

---

*Licensees must only use orchestrations of "Hail to the Chief" that are in the public domain.

ROLAND. Who are you calling a creep? Where is my dear brother anyway?

PENELOPE. That's just it – he's disappeared. His campaign manager thinks he's been abducted!

ROLAND. *(Amused.)* Abducted? By who? Aliens?

PENELOPE. Stay where you are, Roland. I've got to find Lorena.

> *(She hustles off upstage right as* **LORENA** *comes in upstage left, takes one look at* **ROLAND**, *and assumes it's* **BREAM**.)

LORENA. Ah, thank God! You're here!

> *(She runs to him and throws her arms around him.)*

ROLAND. *(A little overwhelmed by the vehemence of her embrace.)* Well, hello! Nice to meet you too!

LORENA. ¿Qué te pasó? ¿Estás bien? [What happened to you? Are you alright?]

ROLAND. *(Enthralled by her use of the language.)* Oh, you speak Spanish! I love Spanish! Say something else!

LORENA. You had me so worried! You can't disappear on me like that without any warning! And what was up with that bizarre message?

ROLAND. Message? Oh crap, I didn't send you one of *those* pictures, did I?

LORENA. Anyway, we can talk about that later. I've got to let everyone know you're back.

> *(Stops, looks at him.)*

I'm just so relieved to have found you. I thought you'd been kidnapped!

> *(She steps in and puts a hand on his shoulder.)*

¡Estaba aterrado! [I was so worried!]

ROLAND. Ooh, I love the way you roll those r's. Sounds like you're purring.

(Making a purring sound.)

Rrrrrrrrrrrrrrr!

(He hugs her a little too enthusiastically, then pinches her bum.)

LORENA. *(Letting out a yelp of surprise.)* ¡Jesús! ¿Qué diablos estás haciendo? [Jesus! What the hell are you doing?]

ROLAND. *(Melting a little.)* Say that again.

LORENA. *(Sniffing.)* Wait a minute – have you been drinking?

ROLAND. No more than usual.

LORENA. *(Incredulous.)* ¿Qué?

ROLAND. *(Imitating her accent.)* "¿Qué?" Sounds like a duck. Quack! Quack! Quack!

*(**PENELOPE** enters downstage right.)*

PENELOPE. Roland! Stop playing the fool.

LORENA. Roland? I thought it was –

(Exasperated.)

Oh, *mierda.*

ROLAND. Sorry to disappoint you.

LORENA. I don't suppose you've seen your brother, have you?

ROLAND. No, Raymond and I tend to travel in different circles.

PENELOPE. *(Remembering.)* Oh my goodness – I know where Raymond is.

LORENA. You do?

PENELOPE. *(Pointing to the quick-change booth.)* I thought he was Roland and I put him in there.

*(**LORENA** dashes over to the booth and throws open the curtain, only to discover that the booth is empty.)*

LORENA. There's no one here.

PENELOPE. *(Looking around.)* Where did he go? I just put him in there a moment ago.

LORENA. Oh God, the press will be here any minute! If he's not here to make that speech, we're going to lose the election!

ROLAND. Wow. Bummer.

LORENA. What are we going to do?

ROLAND. Too bad he doesn't have an understudy.

PENELOPE. Oh my goodness – understudy. That's it!

LORENA. That's what?

PENELOPE. That's what we're going to do. If he doesn't show up, Roland can do it.

ROLAND. What, his press conference?

PENELOPE. Yes.

LORENA. NO!

PENELOPE. What choice do we have? Desperate times and all that.

LORENA. *(Uncertain.)* Oh, I don't know.

ROLAND. Are you out of your minds? I'm having enough trouble keeping my end up in *The Vicar's Knickers*!

PENELOPE. Don't worry, it'll be easy. Come on, Roland. You're an actor. The best actor I know.

LORENA. He won't even have to learn any lines. He can just read it off the Teleprompter!
     (To **ROLAND.***)* Besides, you won't be alone. Our chief scientist, Doctor Zingel, will be standing right beside you. If anyone asks any questions, just let him do the talking.

ROLAND. Come on. Be serious. Who's gonna believe for five seconds that I'm Raymond?

     *(***WHITING*** staggers in from downstage right, shirt unbuttoned, hair a mess, lipstick smeared all over his face.)*

WHITING. Ah, Congressman. There you are.

PENELOPE. Mr. Whiting. I see you and Mandy have been getting acquainted.

WHITING. *(Embarrassed.)* You could call it that. Sorry, I just need a few minutes to...tidy myself up. Where's the bathroom?

PENELOPE. Just down the hall on your left.

(He staggers off the way he came.)

(Calling after him.) Careful with the door. It tends to stick.

ROLAND. Who the hell was that guy?

LORENA. That's not important. What is important is that he thought you were your brother – just like everyone else will!

ROLAND. Forget it. Me handle a press conference? It's never gonna happen.

PENELOPE. Please, Roland, you have to. Not just for your brother's sake, but for the future of the country.

LORENA. And the future of Port Pilchard.

ROLAND. Huh?

LORENA. One of the things your brother was going to announce this afternoon is that he's planning on building a huge P.U. processing plant right here. He's going to put the whole town back to work.

ROLAND. That's great. But I'm not your guy. I don't have what it takes. And between you and me –
(In a super-loud whisper.) I've had a couple of drinks this afternoon.

LORENA. Roland, look, I'm not asking you to be president. I'm just asking you to get through the afternoon. Your brother will turn up sooner or later, and when he does, he can take over.

ROLAND. What's in it for me?

LORENA. *(Losing her patience.)* Ay cabron, ¿qué tu pasa? [What is WITH you, you idiot?]

ROLAND. *(Smitten.)* Say that again.

LORENA. ¿Qué? ¿Qué dije? [What? What did I say?]

ROLAND. Oh, yeah, that's it. Talk Spanish to me, baby.

LORENA. *(Getting it, playing along.)* Oh, ¿te gusta, no? [Oh, you like that, do you?]

ROLAND. Yeah, me gusto alright. More! More!

LORENA. *(Stroking his cheek.)* I tell you what, Roland – do this for me, and I'll give you my private number. You can call me and I'll talk Spanish to you any time you like.

ROLAND. Really?

LORENA. Te lo prometo. [I promise.]

ROLAND. *(A beat, excited like a little boy.)* Can we do it on Skype?

LORENA. Whatever you like.

ROLAND. In that case – I'll do it.

LORENA. You will?

ROLAND. Si. I mean yes.

LORENA. ¡Excelente! ¡Muchas gracias!

(She gives him a big kiss on the cheek as **PENELOPE** *applauds her approval.)*

PENELOPE. Bravo!

*(***WHITING** *yells from offstage downstage right.)*

WHITING. *(Offstage.)* Help! This door is stuck! Get me out of here!

ROLAND. Who *is* that?

LORENA. It's Whiting. The reporter.

(Remembering.)

Oh, *mierda*! He wants to interview you.

ROLAND. Me?

LORENA. No, not you...exactly. Your brother.

ROLAND. Hey, wait a minute – you didn't say anything about an interview!

LORENA. Please, you must do it. It's going to win your brother the election.

WHITING. *(Offstage, banging on the door.)* HEY!!

ROLAND. But what am I supposed to talk about?

LORENA. It's no big deal. He just wants to see that fuel sample and ask you a few questions about the process.

ROLAND. What, P.U.? I don't know anything about that crap!

PENELOPE. Well, improvise. You're an actor, aren't you?

LORENA. No he can't do that. You have to stick to the script.

ROLAND. What script?

LORENA. *(Pulling out her phone and showing him the screen.)* The technical aspects of the process.

ROLAND. I don't know the first thing about that stuff.

> *(Looking at the screen.)*

What do you expect me to do – read this off the screen?

LORENA. Um...

PENELOPE. I know! We can give him the earpiece!

LORENA. Earpiece? What do you mean?

PENELOPE. *(To* **ROLAND.***)* You remember, Roland, that earpiece we gave you during the *Count of Monte Cristo*.

ROLAND. Oh, that was so unnecessary. So I improvised a couple of lines.

PENELOPE. A couple of lines? You "improvised" the whole of Act One!

LORENA. How does it work, this earpiece?

PENELOPE. The stage manager feeds him his lines through a microphone and he repeats what he hears. It works a treat.

ROLAND. I don't know, Pen. Remember what happened when we started picking up the taxi dispatcher.

> *(He giggles.)*

PENELOPE. *(Impatiently.)* That only happened the once.

WHITING. *(Pounding on the bathroom door, offstage.)* Hey? Is there anybody out there?

LORENA. It'll have to do.

WHITING. *(More pounding.)* HEEEEEEEEEY!!!

PENELOPE. What about our reporter?

MANDY. *(Offstage.) I'll get you out, Mr. Whiting!*

WHITING. *(Offstage.)* You stay the hell away from me, Miss Man-handle or whatever your name is!

LORENA. OK, you go get the earpiece. I'm going to run out to the bus and get the sample.

      *(**PENELOPE** exits downstage right.)*

ROLAND. Lorena, I can't do this!

LORENA. *(Stroking his cheek as he starts to melt.)* Coraje, querido. ¡Estarás brillante! [Courage, my dear. You'll be brilliant!]

      (She exits through upstage center.)

ROLAND. Spanish courage isn't going to cut it. I think I need a little of the Dutch variety.

      (He crosses to the boot, pulls out the bottle, takes a few steps downstage.)

    ¡Salud!

      *(He takes a long slug of whiskey as **GILL** and **SHARKEY** enter from upstage right. They freeze as soon as they see him. **GILL** pulls out the tranq gun and takes careful aim at **ROLAND**'s backside when **PENELOPE** comes in from downstage right.)*

PENELOPE. Oh, Mr. Postlethwaite! Mr. Dickey-Dennis!

ROLAND. *(Turning at the sound of **PENELOPE**'s voice and seeing **GILL** and **SHARKEY**.)* Hey, fellas.

PENELOPE. *(Seeing the gun, to **GILL** and **SHARKEY**.)* What on Earth are you doing?

SHARKEY. *(Adopting an English accent.)* Target practice.

      *(**GILL** smacks him.)*

PENELOPE. Target practice?

GILL. *(Adopting his British accent.)* Oh, don't mind Roger, Ms. Witherspoon. He's such a kidder. Actually, we're working on a bit of business for our new play.

PENELOPE. Ooh. Is it another farce?

SHARKEY. No. It's a murder mystery.

PENELOPE. What's it called?

SHARKEY. Umm...

GILL. Murder in the Knockerage. Knickerage. Vicarage.

PENELOPE. *(Crossing to GILL.)* That's an exotic-looking weapon.

> *(She takes it from him and has a closer look.)*

GILL. Yes, it shoots silently! We're planning on using it as our murder weapon.

PENELOPE. *(Admiring the weapon.)* It sounds fascinating. You'll have to send us a draft when it's done. Anyway, sorry to hurry you, but Congressman Bream is about to do a very important interview back here. Would you mind making yourselves scarce for a bit?

> *(Crossing to the emergency exit and opening the door.)*

There's a coffee shop just across the alley.

GILL. But I – we –

SHARKEY. We don't drink coffee actually...

PENELOPE. *(Hustling them out, as they protest.)* Not to worry, they have tea. Of course it's *American* tea, which is hardly the same, but I'm sure you'll make do. Thanks for being so understanding. I really appreciate it.

> *(She closes the door and realizes she still has the tranq gun.)*

Oh, wait, you forgot your – never mind.

> *(She puts the gun on the props table.* **LORENA** *enters through the upstage center door, carrying a large tampon box.)*
>
> *(Seeing the tampon box.)*

What do you plan on doing with those?

LORENA. Pardon?

> *(Looking down at the box.)*

Oh, sorry. It's the P.U. sample. We needed a safe place to hide it.

PENELOPE. Good thinking. That's the last place anyone would look.

LORENA. Exactly what we thought.

> (*She pulls out a litre-sized jar of whiskey-colored liquid from the box and stashes the box out of sight.*)

PENELOPE. And Roland, I've got your earpiece right here.

ROLAND. Right ear? I'd prefer the left.

> (*He laughs uproariously.* **PENELOPE** *and* **LORENA** *roll their eyes.* **PENELOPE** *gives him the earpiece and he fits it in his ear.*)

LORENA. (*Examining it.*) Looks just like a hearing aid.

ROLAND. (*In a loud voice.*) What did you say?

> (*He laughs again. Silence from* **PENELOPE** *and* **LORENA**.)

PENELOPE. (*To* **LORENA**.) Maybe this isn't such a good idea.

LORENA. Too late to back out now. Where's the microphone?

PENELOPE. At the back of the auditorium. Molly will show you where.

(*Calling out.*) Molly! Are you out there?

MOLLY. (*Offstage, on the Tannoy.*) Yeah?

> (**LORENA** *exits through one of the doors upstage center.*)

PENELOPE. Can you test Roland's earpiece for us?

MOLLY. (*On Tannoy.*) Sure thing.

> (**ROLAND** *suddenly leaps to his feet, screaming and yanking the earpiece out of his ear.*)

ROLAND. AAAAGGGHHHHH!!! What are you trying to do, deafen me?

MOLLY. (*On Tannoy.*) Sorry Roland. I'll turn it down a bit.

ROLAND. Thank you.

PENELOPE. *(Heading toward the downstage right exit.)* Right. Sit yourself down. I'll go rescue Mr. Whiting.

MANDY. *(Offstage.) Stop pushing, Mr. Whiting. You have to pull!*

WHITING. *(Offstage.)* That's not what you said earlier!

PENELOPE. *(Offstage.)* Thank you Mandy, I'll take it from here. And for heaven's sake, go and put on some clothes!

ROLAND. Ah, who am I kidding? I can't do this... Screw it – I'm outta here.

> *(He gets up and begins to cross toward the emergency exit when something stops him in his tracks. He slowly turns front, and we see the look of ecstasy on his face as **LORENA** says something Spanish in his ear.)*

(Listening.) Ah, si...si, querida...more, more!

> *(Giggling, he crosses back to the chair and sits down. **PENELOPE** enters from downstage right, followed by a grumpy **WHITING**.)*

WHITING. *(To **PENELOPE**.)* That woman's insatiable. Doesn't she have an off switch?

PENELOPE. Right this way, Mr. Whiting. The congressman is waiting.

WHITING. Are we going to talk back here?

PENELOPE. Yes, it's much more private. The media are starting to arrive out front.

WHITING. *(Crossing to **ROLAND** and sitting down next to him.)* Right then. Well, here we are, at long last. I was beginning to think you were going to renege on our deal.

ROLAND. Who, me? Not a chance. So...did you have fun with Mandy?
(With a wink.) Did she show you her "Hello Kitty" tattoo?

(He grimaces and puts a hand to his ear as **LORENA** *screams something at him in the earpiece.)*

Ow!!!

WHITING. What is it?

ROLAND. Nothing. Just a little…ear worm.

WHITING. I see.

(Turning on the voice recorder on his phone.)

OK, we're recording. Now –

*(***WHITING*** is about to begin the interview when* **PENELOPE** *takes a seat right next to him. He looks at her. A beat.)*

PENELOPE. Oh, don't mind me! Just pretend I'm not here.

WHITING. *(Looking at her dubiously.)* OK…

(Turning to **ROLAND***.)*

Now, Congressman Bream, as you know, the Weever administration has been claiming for months that your energy plan is a fantasy. They've even gone so far as to question your sanity. You claim to have proof that P.U. works. So let's hear it.

(A beat, as **ROLAND** *listens to Lorena's response.)*

ROLAND. *(To Lorena.)* Sorry? Could you repeat that?

WHITING. *(Loudly.)* I said, you claim to have proof that P.U. works.

ROLAND. *(To* **WHITING***.)* No, I heard you fine.

WHITING. Huh? So I was asking you to –

ROLAND. *(Obviously listening to Lorena.)* Right. Got it. OK. Here's the thing:

(Unconsciously parroting Lorena's Hispanic accent.)

De problem weet de P.U. process iss dat eet alwayss took more energy to produce de fuel dan de fuel produced eetself. Finally, Doctor Zingel found a way around dis hurdle and solved de problem.

(**WHITING** *looks at him curiously.* **PENELOPE** *puts her face in her hands.*)

WHITING. Congressman Bream, is there some reason you're talking like Speedy Gonzales?

ROLAND. Am I? ...

(*Listening to Lorena.*)

I did? ...Oh, I didn't mean to... Well that's how you pronounced it!

WHITING. Congressman, are you OK?

ROLAND. (*DJ voice as the radio frequency kicks in.*) And this just in – there's a fender bender southbound on Highway Fifty-Two. Traffic's backed up so you might want to avoid the area for the next little while. Coming up next on Oldies FM, one of the biggest hits of the seventies...

(*Reacting to painful feedback in his ear.*)

Ow!

PENELOPE. You'll have to excuse him, Mr. Whiting. He slipped and hit his head getting off the bus this afternoon.

WHITING. (*Suspicious.*) Really? He seemed fine when I talked with him earlier.

PENELOPE. Oh, this just happened. The doctor says he's suffered a mild concussion.

WHITING. I'm sorry to hear that.

PENELOPE. Yes, he's really not himself right now.

ROLAND. (*Chuckling.*) You can say that again!

(*Listening to Lorena as she gives him shit, then to* **WHITING.**)

SMARTEN UP!

WHITING. Huh?

ROLAND. (*Listening, then to* **WHITING.**) Oh. Sorry. Not you.

PENELOPE. (*To* WHITING, *apologetically.*) See what I mean?

> (ROLAND *smiles placidly at* WHITING, *then suddenly launches very loudly into a disco tune.** *He continues singing for a bit until painful feedback stops him short.*)

ROLAND. (*Holding his ear.*) Ow!

> (*He turns to* WHITING *and smiles pathetically.*)

WHITING. (*Beat.*) Anyway, where were we?

> (*Consulting his notes.*)

Oh yes – the process. Now, you claim that P.U. is not only a viable fuel source, but that it's sustainable, non-polluting and will be less expensive than conventional fuels. Do you have any proof to back that up?

ROLAND. (*Listening.*) I have fat fingers... I have the fat and fingers...huh?

> (*As the penny finally drops, excitedly.*)

Oh, the FACTS AND FIGURES!

> (*Overcome with joy that he's finally deciphered what Lorena has said.*)

I HAVE THE FACTS AND FIGURES!!

> (WHITING *recoils from this outburst.*)

PENELOPE. Maybe that concussion isn't quite as mild as we thought...

WHITING. Let's talk about Weever's claims that this fuel is going to make everyone's car smell "like a tuna fish sandwich."

ROLAND. (*Laughing.*) Yeah, that commercial with the cats is a scream.

---

*A license to produce *Something Fishy* does not include a performance license for any third-party or copyrighted music. Licensees should create an original composition or use music in the public domain. For further information, please see Music Use Note on page 3.

(He laughs some more, then snaps out of it as Lorena berates him through the earpiece. He instantly adopts a serious, ministerial tone and continues:)

And totally inaccurate. And I can prove it to you... Show him the jar.

WHITING. Pardon?

ROLAND. *(Listening.)* Oh, me! Right. I'm going to show you the fuel right now.

WHITING. Really? You've brought a sample? Where is it?

ROLAND. *(Listening.)* Right underneath you.

WHITING. What?

ROLAND. Oh, right underneath *me*! Sorry.

(He looks under his chair, pulls out the jar, and hands it to **WHITING**.*)*

Take a whiff.

WHITING. *(Unscrewing the jar and taking a sniff.)* Hmm. You're right. Doesn't smell like fish at all. In fact –

(Taking another sniff.)

It kinda smells like whiskey.

ROLAND. *(Intrigued.)* Really?

(He snatches the jar from **WHITING** *and takes a healthy sniff himself.)*

You're right. It does.

(He takes a gulp. **WHITING** *and* **PENELOPE** *gasp in horror.)*

Whoa! That stuff's got quite a kick to it!

(He's about to take another sip when **PENELOPE** *swoops in and takes the jar away from him. Meanwhile,* **ROLAND**'s *attention becomes fixed as he listens to Lorena ranting at him in Spanish.)*

(Enraptured, clearly titillated by what he's hearing.)

ROLAND. Oh si, si, querida... Oh, I love it when you talk dirty to me...

WHITING. *(Standing up.)* OK, what the hell is going on here?

PENELOPE. Like I said, he's had a head injury.

WHITING. Head injury nothing. Weever is right – this guy is certifiable.

> *(LORENA comes barreling in, panting, through one of the doors upstage center.)*

LORENA. Mr. Whiting, please, let me explain –

WHITING. There's nothing to explain.

> *(Holding up his phone.)*

I've got all I need right here.

> *(Pointing to ROLAND.)*

That guy's nuts, and I'm going to tell the world all about it!

> *(He starts to leave.)*

LORENA. You can't do that!

WHITING. Oh no? Just watch me. I've even got the perfect headline – Bream's Fried – In His Own Fish Oil!

> *(He turns to exit. As he does so, PENELOPE, in an act of desperation, picks up the tranq gun and points it at him.)*

PENELOPE. Hold it right there, Buster!

> *(She shoots him in the rear. He drops to the floor. PENELOPE screams. A beat. ROLAND and LORENA slowly turn to PENELOPE, amazed.)*

ROLAND. Nice shootin', Pen.

PENELOPE. Oh dear lord, what have I done?

LORENA. You may have just saved our lives.

> *(She crosses to WHITING, checks his pulse, etc.)*

PENELOPE. *(Tremulously.)* Is he...?

LORENA. He's fine. He's just unconscious.

(Holding up a dart.)

It's a tranquilizer gun.

PENELOPE. Oh thank God.

LORENA. *(Looking around, finally spotting the quick-change booth.)* Quick – we've got to get him out of sight. Let's put him in here.

ROLAND. I'll take care of it.

> *(He hauls* **WHITING** *into the quick-change booth.)*

PENELOPE. What do we do now?

LORENA. It's fine. We're fine. Roland can do the speech as planned, and we can track down señor Bream.

PENELOPE. What do we do about Whiting?

LORENA. We'll deal with him later.

PENELOPE. I'd better wipe my prints off this gun.

> *(She carefully wipes the gun on her skirt, then sets it back on the props table. She looks to the quick-change booth.)*

Are you sure Roland is up for this?

LORENA. No, but he's all we've got.

MOLLY. *(Offstage.) Pen, can I let the people in now? The lobby is packed.*

PENELOPE. One moment, Molly. I'll be right with you!
(To **LORENA**.*) What should I do about the press?*

LORENA. Stall them. I need a few minutes.

PENELOPE. You've got it.

LORENA. Oh – and if you happen to run into Doctor Zingel, could you send him back here?

PENELOPE. Of course. How will I know him?

LORENA. Oh, you'll know him. He looks like the mad scientist from every fifties sci-fi movie ever made. And he speaks with a German accent.

PENELOPE. Of course he does.

> *(She exits upstage right.)*

LORENA. *(Calling.)* Roland, are you OK in there?

ROLAND. *(From inside the quick-change booth.)* Yeah, just having a little trouble getting this guy organized. I'll be with you in a minute.

> (**LORENA** *crosses to put the fuel jar back in the tampon box. As she does this,* **BREAM,** *dressed in the vicar's cassock and hat, enters from the upstage left door and crosses toward the quick-change booth. He's still suffering from the aftereffects of the tranquilizer.* **LORENA** *turns back, sees him, and assumes it's* **ROLAND.**)

LORENA. What are you doing in that ridiculous outfit? Take it off!

> *(She crosses to him and starts pulling off the cassock, collar, and hat.* **BREAM,** *still disoriented, allows her to do this, occasionally poking his head like a pigeon and cooing.)*

Stop fooling around! I've had enough of you. Don't you realize what's at stake here? This isn't just about your brother's future – it's about the future of the country!

BREAM. My brother?

LORENA. Oh, I know you don't care about him. If you did, you wouldn't have made such a mess of that interview. Drinking the P.U. What were you thinking?

BREAM. Drink? I could use a drink. I'm absolutely parched.

LORENA. I think you've had quite enough to drink for one day, thank you.

> *(He begins pecking at the buttons on her blouse.)*
>
> *(Recoiling.)*

Ay, stop that! What's wrong with you?

> (**BREAM** *thrusts his head like a pigeon, cooing again a few times.)*

That's what you get for drinking the P.U. *Dios mio*, we can't have you going out in front of the press like this. Come on – let's see if some fresh air does you any good.

*(She escorts him to the emergency exit. **BREAM** dutifully follows, pecking and cooing as he goes. As they exit, **GILL** and **SHARKEY** enter through the door upstage center.)*

GILL. Shit, now where did he get to?

(A few grunts are heard emanating from the quick-change booth.)

ROLAND. *(Offstage.)* Geez, now I know what they mean by "dead weight"!

*(**GILL** and **SHARKEY** wheel around toward the quick-change booth.)*

*(**SHARKEY** points toward it as **GILL** crosses to the props table and picks up the tranq gun.)*

SHARKEY. *(Sotto voce.)* He's in there!

*(At that moment, **ROLAND**'s [a body double's] butt pokes through the curtains. **GILL** takes aim and shoots. **ROLAND** drops, his butt still poking through the curtains.)*

GILL. I better hit him again, just to be safe.

(He fires a couple more times.)

SHARKEY. Easy there, big guy.

*(**SHARKEY** takes the gun from **GILL** and pockets it.)*

GILL. Now – let's get his ass out of here.

*(They start to cross toward the quick-change booth just as **MANDY** enters from the dressing rooms.)*

MANDY. Well, if it isn't my two favorite British playwrights!

SHARKEY. *(Under his breath.)* Oh, God.

> *(They quickly shove* **ROLAND** *back into the quick-change booth and close the curtains.)*

GILL. *(Affecting the British accent.)* Well, if it isn't Ms. Randall!

MANDY. *(Crossing to him.)* Ah-ah-ah-ah! It's Mandy, remember?

GILL. Of course – Mandy.

MANDY. *(Flirtatiously.)* And may I call you Crispy?

GILL. I don't know; sounds a little – overdone.

MANDY. I assume you've come back to hear the congressman's speech?

SHARKEY. *(Horrified, no accent.)* Oh God, no!

GILL. *(Covering for him.)* Uh, no. Politics isn't really our thing.

MANDY. No, me neither.

> *(Seductively.)* I can think of a much more interesting way to pass the time.

SHARKEY. Sorry love, but I'm afraid we don't play for the same team.

MANDY. I don't mind what team you play for, I'm a "free agent."

> **(SHARKEY** *and* **GILL** *look at each other.)*

Tell me, have you ever been with a woman?

SHARKEY. *(Stumped.)* Umm…

GILL. *(Coming to the rescue.)* No, actually, and I've always been a bit curious.

> **(SHARKEY** *looks at him, surprised.* **GILL** *waves him off.)*

MANDY. Well you know what they say about curiosity, Crispy.

GILL. That it killed the cat?

MANDY. Uh-huh. Feel like spending one of your nine lives?

GILL. Oh, why not?

SHARKEY. What?

GILL. Don't be jealous, darling.

(*To* **MANDY**.) He's *so* possessive.

(**SHARKEY** *looks at him quizzically.*)

Although he has no right to be. He has a few –

(*Gesturing toward the quick-change booth.*)

Skeletons of his own in the closet.

SHARKEY. Huh?

GILL. (*To* **MANDY**.) Now, why don't you go and get yourself ready. Roger and I just need to umm…work a few things out and I'll be right behind you.

MANDY. Oh no. I can't risk Roger softening your resolve.

(*Grabbing* **GILL**'s *hand.*)

Let's go now while it's still firm.

(*She begins to drag him off downstage right. As he goes,* **GILL** *looks at* **SHARKEY** *and gestures to the quick-change booth and the emergency door.* **SHARKEY** *finally gets it.*)

SHARKEY. (*Thumbs up.*) Right!

(**SHARKEY** *crosses to the quick-change booth and looks inside.*)

Hey, who's this other guy? Oh well, not my problem…

(*He bends down and is about to haul* **ROLAND** *out of the quick-change booth when* **MOLLY** *enters from the upstage right door.*)

MOLLY. (*Looking around.*) Lorena, are you back here?

(*At the sound of her voice,* **SHARKEY** *immediately stands and affects an air of nonchalance.*)

Oh, Mr. Dickey-Dennis. Where did everybody go? The press are here. We have to get started.

SHARKEY. (*British accent.*) So sorry darling, I haven't seen a soul.

MOLLY. Oh, dear. And there's a fella looking for Lorena. He says it's important.

> *(She exits back through the upstage right door.* **SHARKEY** *goes to drag* **ROLAND** *out again when* **DR. ZINGEL** *enters through the upstage left door. Behind him, we hear the sound of the crowd taking their seats in the auditorium.* **ZINGEL** *is dressed in a white lab coat and glasses, and has a mop of unruly, grey, Einstein-like hair. He speaks with a German accent.)*

ZINGEL. Gut afternoon.

SHARKEY. *(Wheeling around.)* Oh! Uh, hello.
(Lapsing into British accent.) How do you do?

> *(Offering his hand.)*

Roger Dickey-Dennis – playwright at large.

ZINGEL. *(Shaking hands.)* Pleased to meet you, Herr Dickey-Dennis. Heilbutt Zingel.

SHARKEY. Wait a minute – you mean Doctor Zingel – the P.U. scientist?

ZINGEL. Ja, zat's me! I'm here to help Herr Bream show my new invention to ze vorld! Tell me, have you seen him anyvere?

SHARKEY. Herr Bream – uh, Congressman Bream?

> *(Takes to the quick-change booth, then unconsciously adopting Zingel's accent:)*

Uh, ya. I beleef he's out in zee lobby.

> *(He points upstage left.)*

ZINGEL. Excellent. Sank you.

> *(As* **ZINGEL** *crosses to the upstage right door,* **SHARKEY** *pulls out the tranq gun and shoots* **ZINGEL** *in the butt.* **ZINGEL** *crumples and* **SHARKEY** *crosses quickly to catch him by the armpits.)*

SHARKEY. Time to haul butt, Heilbutt...

> (*He drags* **ZINGEL** *to the quick-change booth and stuffs him inside.*)

Getting awful crowded in here. Come on, Bream, let's get out of this madhouse.

> (*He then takes hold of* **ROLAND** *and is about to drag him out of the booth when* **GILL** *rushes on from downstage right in his shirtsleeves and underwear, followed by an irate* **PENELOPE**, *who holds his pants in her hand.*)

GILL. (*No accent.*) Please, it's not what you think!

PENELOPE. When it comes to Mandy, it's always what I think!

GILL. It wasn't my idea – she forced me into it!

PENELOPE. Oh please. You were panting for it.

GILL. Uh, speaking of pants, would you mind?

> (*He puts out a hand to* **PENELOPE**. *She holds on to the pants.*)

PENELOPE. Wait a moment – what's happened to your accent? Who are you two anyway?

GILL. (*Trying to recover his British accent.*) You know who we are. I'm...er...er...Crispy...Micklewhite and he's Roger Dickey-Dumplings!

PENELOPE. Who do you think you're kidding? Let's just see what your ID says.

> (*Pulling* **GILL***'s wallet out of his pants.*)

Oh, so tell me Mr. "Micklewhite," what are you doing with a Maryland driver's license?

(*Reading.*) "Robert Gill."

SHARKEY. (*Pulling out the tranq gun.*) Looks like we're going to have to shoot another one.

> (*He takes aim and shoots. Nothing happens. He checks the gun.*)

Shit. I'm empty.

SHARKEY. *(To* GILL.*)* Grab her!

> (GILL *makes a move toward* PENELOPE, *who races out the upstage right door.* GILL *follows her as far as the open doorway, spots the crowd in the auditorium, and immediately turns to run back in. He trips and falls, his butt facing the assembled throng. Behind him, camera flashes go off by the dozen. He gets up quickly, slams the door, then crosses sheepishly downstage center.)*

GILL. Oh my God. My ass is going to be on the cover of every newspaper in the country.

SHARKEY. Well, let's cover both our asses and get out of here!

GILL. How can I? I have no pants!

SHARKEY. *(Pointing at the quick-change booth.)* Grab Bream's.

GILL. That'll work.

> *(He crosses to the quick-change booth and looks inside.)*

Holy crap, who are all these guys?

SHARKEY. The guy in the lab coat is Doctor Zingel.

GILL. That's Zingel?

SHARKEY. Yup. Bagged him myself.

GILL. Good job.

> (MOLLY *enters upstage left.)*

MOLLY. Oh, hello.

> *(Seeing* GILL *has no pants.)*

What's happened to your pants, Mr. Postlethwaite?

GILL. *(To* SHARKEY.*)* Postlethwaite, damn! I was close.

MOLLY. I beg your pardon?

GILL. *(Remembering his accent this time.)* Oh, nothing. We're just working on some stage business.

MOLLY. Looks more like monkey business to me.

(She laughs, briefly, at her joke.)

Have you seen Doctor Zingel? Someone said he came back here.

*(**GILL** and **SHARKEY** take to the quick-change booth.)*

GILL & SHARKEY. No, sorry, no doctors here.

MOLLY. Well, if you do see him, please tell him to stay put, would you?

GILL. Righty-o. Will do.

*(**MOLLY** exits upstage left.)*

OK, you get Bream and Zingel out of that booth while I find something to wear.

SHARKEY. Oh, no you don't. I'm not hauling these guys around by myself.

GILL. Alright, stop whining. I'll give you a hand.

*(They cross to the quick-change booth and haul **ROLAND** out onto the floor. At that moment, the emergency door opens and a severe-looking woman enters, dressed in a conservative business suit. **SHARKEY** turns and spots her first.)*

SHARKEY. President Weever!

WEEVER. There you are!

GILL. Madam President!

WEEVER. Yes, you idiot, we've established that.

*(Noticing **GILL** has no pants.)*

What are you doing in your underwear?

GILL. It's a long story.

SHARKEY. *(Under his breath, with a look to **GILL**'s undies.)* Not as long as it was a few minutes ago...

GILL. *(Sotto voce.)* Shut up!

WEEVER. Never mind. I've heard enough out of you two for one day. You've been selling me a bill of goods ever since that fiasco in Pussy Creek this morning.

GILL. I can explain that –

WEEVER. Everything you've told me today has been a pack of lies. I show up here believing that Raymond Bream has been taken care of and what's the first thing I see? Raymond Bream taking a stroll around the parking lot with his campaign manager!

GILL. That's impossible. He's right here.

> (*He and* **SHARKEY** *show her the comatose* **ROLAND**. **WEEVER** *crosses over to him to get a better look.*)

WEEVER. I don't understand. I just saw him outside not fifteen seconds ago.

SHARKEY. It can't be him. He's been stuffed in that booth there for the last half hour – along with his buddy Zingel.

WEEVER. What? Doctor Zingel's here?

SHARKEY. Yes, but don't worry – I took care of him as well.

WEEVER. What is Bream doing here in the first place? You bozos told me he was sleeping it off in some motel!

GILL. He was! He just didn't sleep quite as long as we expected.

WEEVER. Oh my God. Get rid of him!

> (**GILL** *and* **SHARKEY** *start to haul* **ROLAND** *to his feet. At that moment,* **LORENA** *enters from the emergency door downstage left.* **GILL** *and* **SHARKEY** *immediately shove* **ROLAND** *into the booth and shut the curtains.*)

LORENA. (*Seeing* **WEEVER**.) Madam President! What are you doing here?

WEEVER. (*Taken aback.*) Oh, uh, well, I was campaigning in the area and, uh, I thought I'd come and hear Bream's speech; however, I understand he's gone missing.

LORENA. (*Surprised to learn that* **WEEVER** *knows this.*) Where did you hear that?

WEEVER. (*With a look to* **GILL** *and* **SHARKEY**.) A little bird told me.

LORENA. Well, I'm afraid your little bird is mistaken.

> *(Pointing toward the emergency door.)*

The congressman is here.

WEEVER. Are you sure about that?

LORENA. Sure I'm sure. He's out in the bus, getting ready to make his presentation – which we're about to do, as soon as I can find Doctor Zingel.

WEEVER. Oh, haven't you heard? Doctor Zingel has disappeared.

LORENA. *(Aghast.)* What??

WEEVER. That's right – Zingel's gone, and he's not coming back.

> *(With a loud flurry of bird-like squawks,*
> **ZINGEL** *enters from the quick-change booth. He*
> *is clearly suffering from the effects of the bird*
> *tranquilizer.)*

ZINGEL. Someone looking for me?

> *(He thrusts his head and squawks.)*

LORENA. Doctor Zingel! I'm so happy to see you!

ZINGEL. Happy to see you too, whoever you are.

> *(He sees something shiny on her clothing and*
> *pecks at it.)*

WEEVER. What's wrong with him?

> *(To* **ZINGEL***.)* What happened to you?

ZINGEL. I haff no idea. I came back here, and ze next sing I knew, I voke up in zat little hut.

LORENA. Oh, don't worry, he'll be fine. I know just what he needs.

> *(Taking* **ZINGEL** *by the hand and urging him*
> *toward the emergency exit.)*

Come along, Doctor Zingel. A little fresh air and you'll be right as rain.

> *(They exit,* **ZINGEL** *strutting like a bird as*
> *they go.)*

WEEVER. What's with the chicken dance?

SHARKEY. Oh, that. We shot him with bird tranquilizer.

WEEVER. Bird tranquilizer??

(**SHARKEY** *and* **GILL** *look at each other.*)

GILL. Well you see, the boys at the Department of Defense —

WEEVER. *(Rubbing her temples.)* I don't want to hear it. Now, this is the plan:
(*To* **GILL**.) You put Bream here in your car,
(*Turning to* **SHARKEY**.) and you get out there and take care of those people on his bus.

SHARKEY. Take care of them? How?

WEEVER. Put them all to sleep with that bird tranquilizer of yours. While they're all napping, drive them off and leave them in the middle of nowhere.
(*Indicating* **GILL**.) Crazy legs here can follow in the car and pick you up when you're done. By the time they wake up they'll have no idea how they got there. Got it?

GILL. Got it.

SHARKEY. *(Loading the tranq gun.)* It's like something out of James Bond.

GILL. What are you going to do, Madam President?

WEEVER. *(Pointing upstage center.)* I'm going to walk in through the front door as if none of this ever happened. When they finally figure out that Bream's not coming, I can step in and make a little speech of my own.

GILL. I can't believe it. It looks like we're actually going to pull this off!

WEEVER. No thanks to you.

SHARKEY. Right. I'm locked and loaded. Time to go bird hunting...

WEEVER. Don't. Mess. This. Up.

SHARKEY. Don't worry, Madam President. You can count on me.

(He exits through the emergency door downstage left.)

GILL. *(Crossing toward the quick-change booth.)* Come along, Bream.

WEEVER. Stop!!

GILL. *(Alarmed.)* What is it?

WEEVER. PLEASE put on some pants. I've seen enough of your tighty whities for one day.

GILL. Oh. Right. Sorry.

(She grabs a pair of loudly patterned plus fours from the rack and throws them at him.)

WEEVER. Here. Put these on.

(He quickly shoves the pants on.)

If the public only knew the lengths I go to...

GILL. We'd all be in prison.

*(Reaching into the quick-change booth and dragging **ROLAND**'s feet through the curtains. [NB: these will be the feet of the actor playing **WHITING**.])*

Alright, let's get you out of here, Bream.

*(As he says this, the emergency door opens and **BREAM** and **LORENA** enter.)*

BREAM. Looking for me?

*(**GILL** and **WEEVER** turn and react with shock. **GILL** drops the feet.)*

GILL. Aagh!!

*(Pointing at **BREAM**.)*

But, but...how can you be there –

*(Pointing at **ROLAND**'s feet.)*

When you're here?

BREAM. *(Crossing to **GILL**.)* I know. It's astounding, isn't it? I'm beside myself.

(Looking down at **ROLAND**'s *feet.)*

BREAM. Literally.

(**ROLAND** *stirs in the booth and coos.*)

ROLAND. *Lady Darlington, where on Earth is my glass of Scotch? Coo! Coo!*

(He draws his feet back into the booth.)

WEEVER. Who is that?

BREAM. Sounds like my brother Roland.

GILL. Your brother?

WEEVER. Of course. That's why we're seeing double.

LORENA. And as for your partner, the one with the tranquilizer gun...

(She holds up the gun.)

BREAM. He's out in the bus in handcuffs. My security people are feeding him bread crumbs.

WEEVER. That idiot.

BREAM. You didn't really think you were going to get away with this scheme, did you, Eva?

WEEVER. Get away with what? I haven't done anything wrong.

LORENA. Oh no? What about kidnapping? And assault? And administering a noxious substance?

WEEVER. I had nothing to do with any of that. Besides, you have no proof. I mean, the president orchestrating a kidnapping? Who's going to believe a ridiculous story like that?

(**WHITING** *steps out of the quick-change booth, holding up his mobile phone and occasionally flapping his arms and tweeting like a bird. This should sound very much like the online Twitter sound effect.*)

WHITING. Me, for one.

(He tweets for a while.)

WEEVER. Who the hell are you?

LORENA. Madam President, may I introduce Mr. Jim Whiting of the RNR.

WHITING. How do you do? Say cheese!

> (**LORENA** *and* **BREAM** *step in behind* **WEEVER** *as* **WHITING** *snaps a picture with his phone and thrusts his head again.*)

There. That's the cover for our next issue. It's going to sell a million copies!

WEEVER. Why? I get my photograph taken with people all the time.

WHITING. Oh, I've got a lot more than just a photograph. Have a look at this –

> (*He clicks a button on his phone and shows it to them. We hear the following coming out of his phone:*)

WEEVER. *You put Bream here in your car, and you get out there and take care of those people on his bus.*

SHARKEY. *Take care of them? How?*

WEEVER. *Put them all to sleep with that bird tranquilizer of yours. While they're all napping, drive them off and leave them in the middle of nowhere.*

> (**WHITING** *clicks off the phone.*)

WHITING. As you can see from the video, President Weever, there's no question that it's you.

WEEVER. You can't publish that!

WHITING. Too late – I've already uploaded it to the RNR website.

GILL. The *Red Neck Report*? I thought you guys were on our side!

WHITING. Hey, a story's a story – and this one's going to make me a star!

WEEVER. (*Collapsing into a chair in defeat.*) Oh my God.

WHITING. Well, I think my work here is done.

(Crossing to **BREAM** *and shaking his hand.)*

WHITING. Good luck out there, sir. Guess I'll see you at the inauguration.

BREAM. I look forward to it. Then I can give you that interview I promised you.

WHITING. Didn't we do that already?

BREAM. Did we?

LORENA. I'll explain later.

WHITING. *(Nodding to* **WEEVER.***)* Madam President.

> *(He thrusts his head, tweeting as he exits through the emergency door. The noise of the assembled multitude in the auditorium increases.)*

LORENA. Congressman? They're waiting. It's time.

BREAM. Right. I'd better get out there.

(To **WEEVER**, *with a smile.)* Care to join me?

WEEVER. *(Stonily.)* No thank you. Come along, Gill.

> *(They begin to cross toward the emergency door.)*

LORENA. Excuse me. I don't believe those pants belong to you.

> *(With one deft move she rips them off.)*

GILL. Aagh!

> *(With as much dignity as he can muster, he crosses to the emergency door in his undies, holds the door open for* **WEEVER**, *and they exit.)*

LORENA. Wow. How's that for irony; the Evil Weevil being brought down by her number one cheerleader – the *Red Neck Report*.

BREAM. Didn't see that one coming. Talk about your karma running over your dogma.

LORENA. *(Looking at him.)* Hey. The pecking. It's stopped.

BREAM. What pecking?

LORENA. I think it was that tranquilizer they shot you with. You've been pecking and cooing like a pigeon all afternoon.

BREAM. Have I? I don't remember. It's all a bit foggy to me. I feel fine now.

LORENA. Just in time, too.

BREAM. *(Taking her hands.)* I want to thank you, Lorena. You really saved my bacon today. I can't imagine what you've had to cope with.

LORENA. Oh, it wasn't that bad. The hardest part was getting your brother to keep his hands off me. Oh Dios mio. Te lo estoy diciendo... [Oh my God. I'm telling you...]

> *(From the quick-change booth, we hear:)*

ROLAND. *Oh, yeah baby! I love it. More! More!*

BREAM. What's that all about?

LORENA. Oh, Roland's got a fetish for Spanish.

BREAM. *(Smiling shyly.)* Is that so? He's not alone, you know.

LORENA. What do you mean?

BREAM. Well we are twins, after all. We do have a few things in common.

> *(Beat.)*

Dime algo en español. [Say something to me in Spanish.]

LORENA. *(Laughing.)* Ah, ¿tu también? ¡Es increible! [Oh, you too? It's incredible!]

> *(BREAM's knees go a little weak at this. He whimpers slightly. From the booth we hear ROLAND do the same.)*

BREAM & ROLAND. *Oh, yeah. That's it.*

BREAM. *(Turning to the booth.)* Keep it down, Roland.

LORENA. *(With a playful slap on BREAM's wrist.)* ¡Suficiente! ¡No es buen momento! [That's enough! This isn't a good time!]

(BREAM and ROLAND whimper again.)

ROLAND. *Si, si. More! More!*

BREAM. *(To the booth.)* Ssh!

LORENA. I can see that the next four years are going to be very interesting...

BREAM. *(Taking her in his arms.)* Yes. And I can see I'm going to need a lot of help with my Spanish.

LORENA. Only too happy to be of assistance.

> *(They are about to kiss when we hear COLIN's voice from offstage.)*

COLIN. *(Offstage.)* Pen, Pen – I did it!

> *(He comes running in from downstage right dressed in full drag – in the dowager outfit he has been trying to put on all day. BREAM and LORENA break apart.)*

Forty-three and half seconds flat!

> *(He spots BREAM and LORENA.)*

Ooh. Sorry. Haven't missed your speech, have I?

LORENA. No, he's just about to start.

COLIN. Great. Break a leg!

> *(He dashes out the door upstage right. At the same time, PENELOPE enters through the door upstage left.)*

PENELOPE. We're ready to go.

BREAM. Coming! Wait a moment – where's Zingel?

PENELOPE. I found him wandering around outside, pecking in the dirt. But don't worry – I gave him a cup of tea and he's fine now. He's waiting for you on stage.

BREAM. Okay, folks. Let's do this.

LORENA. Penelope, would you mind doing the introduction?

PENELOPE. *(Thrilled.)* Oh, I'd be honored! Now?

LORENA. Yes please.

> *(Gesturing to the door.)*

After you.

> (**PENELOPE** *and* **LORENA** *exit through the upstage left door.* **BREAM** *takes a breath, crosses to the quick-change booth, and opens the curtain a crack.*)

BREAM. Thanks, Roland.

> (*Rubbing his sore bum.*)

You saved my butt big time. I don't know how I'll ever pay you back.

ROLAND. *You could always make me Secretary of State.*

BREAM. (*Laughs.*) Deal!

PENELOPE. (*On mic.*) Ladies and gentlemen, it gives me great pleasure to introduce you to the next President of the United States, Congressman Raymond Bream!

> (**BREAM** *walks through the upstage center door to a round of thunderous applause. He waves to the crowd and closes the door.*)

BREAM. (*On mic.*) *Ladies and gentlemen, members of the press, and citizens of the greatest town in the country, my home town of Port Pilchard. I want to thank you all for coming here today.*

> (**ROLAND** *emerges from the quick-change booth, retrieves his bottle from the usual spot, and while listening to his brother's speech, grabs a plastic cup off the props table and pours a healthy measure. He is still suffering the effects of the bird tranquilizer.*)

There's been a lot of controversy in the press recently about my energy policy. My opponent, President Weever, says P.U. won't work, that it's going to make the country smell like fish. Well, today Doctor Zingel and I are going to prove her wrong!

> (*Thunderous applause.*)

BREAM. *(On mic.) I guarantee that when we're finished here this afternoon, the only thing you'll be smelling in Port Pilchard will be the sweet smell of success!!*

> *(A huge round of applause comes from the front of house as* **ROLAND** *raises his cup, honking like a bird, and begins to peck at it in an attempt to take a drink. The lights fade to black.)*

End of Play

Canadian Version Addendum

ACT I

CHARACTER CHANGE

Actor 2's character Lorena: change to Josée. Character is now French Canadian.

Actor 3's character Penelope: changes from a "Southern Belle" to a "Brit."

Pg. 7 In the set description: change "Ohio" to "Ontario."

Pg. 8 Set description, first paragraph: Change "Presidential" to "federal."

Pg. 12 Colin's first speech: lose the first capitalized "Congressman" and change the second one to "Mr." Also, change "President" to "Prime Minister" and lose "race to the White House."

Pg. 13 Penelope's fourth speech: change "the Congressman's" to "Raymond's."

Pg. 16 Clark's final speech: change the lower-case "president" to "prime minister" (global change).

Pg. 17 Judy's fifth speech: change "President's" to "Prime Minister's."

Colin's fourth speech: change "Washington" to "Ottawa."

Pg. 20 Molly's first speech: change "Secret Service" to "RCMP (global change).

Pg. 21 Molly's fifth speech: change "Dunkin' Donuts" to "Tim Horton's" (global change).

Pg. 22 Penelope's first speech: change "Congressman" to "Mr."

Pg. 23 Bream's first speech: change "the tenth grade" to "grade ten."

Pg. 24 Josée's (Lorena's) second speech: change "the Congressman" to "Mr. Bream."

Pg. 26 Josée's (Lorena's) last speech: change "Dices bien" to "Touché."

Whiting's first speech: change "Congressman" to "Mr."

Josée's (Lorena's) last speech: change "Buen Dios!" to "Seigneur!"

Pg. 28 Bream's fourth speech: change "President" to "Prime Minister."

Pg. 29 Whiting's fifth speech: change "Congressman" to "Mr."

Josée's (Lorena's) first speech: change "Congressman" to "Mr. Bream."

Pg. 33 Gill's fifth speech: change "President" to "Prime Minister."

Stage direction in same speech: change "Hail to the Chief" to "O Canada."

Same speech (after "answering phone"): change "President" to "Prime Minister."

Pg. 34 Gill's first speech: change "President" to "Prime Minister."

Sharkey's second speech: change "President" to "Prime Minsiter."

Pg. 37 Penelope's fourth speech: change "President" to "Prime Minister."

Pg. 38 Molly's second speech: change "the Congressman's" to "Mr. Bream's."

Pg. 40 Gill's second speech: change "President" to "Prime Minister."

Pg. 46 Molly's first speech: change "Congressman" to "Mr. Bream."

Pg. 49 Gill's third speech: change "Spanish terrier" to "French bulldog."

ACT II

Pg. 65	Roland's first speech: change the entire line "Oh, I love the way you..." to the following: "That's it, baby! Purr for me! Purr, purr, purrrrrrrr!"
Pg. 65	Josée's (Lorena's) second speech: change "¡Jesús! ¿Qué diablos estás haciendo?" to "Câlisse! Qu'est-ce que tu fais tabarnak?"
Pg. 65	Josée's (Lorena's) fifth speech: change "mierda" to "merde" (global change).
Pg. 67	Whiting's first speech: change "Congressman" to "Mr. Bream."
Pg. 67	Josée's (Lorena's) last speech: change "President" to "Prime Minister."
Pg. 68	Josée's (Lorena's) first speech: change "Ay cabron, ¿qué tu pasa? [What is WITH you, you idiot?]" to "Maudit merde! Qu'est-ce que tu veux, tabarnak? [Goddamn shit! What do you want, dammit?]"
Pg. 68	Josée's (Lorena's) second speech: change "¿Que dije?" to "Qu'est-ce que j'ai dit?"
Pg. 68	Josée's (Lorena's) third speech: change "Oh, ¿te gusta, no?" to "Oh, t'aimes ça, hein?"
Pg. 68	Roland's fourth speech: change "Yeah, me gusto alright." to "Yeah, that's it."
Pg. 68	Josée's (Lorena's) fifth speech: change "Te lo prometo" to "Je te promets."
Pg. 68	Roland's eighth speech: change "Si" to "Oui."
Pg. 68	Josée's (Lorena's) eighth speech: change "¡Excelente! ¡Muchas gracias!" to "Oh, oui. (In French) Excellent! Merçi beaucoup!"
Pg. 70	Josée's (Lorena's) third speech: change "Coraje, querido. ¡Estarás brillante!" to "Courage, chéri. Tu seras formidable!"
Pg. 70	Roland's third speech: change "¡Salud!" to "Salut!"
Pg. 71	Penelope's sixth speech: change "Congressman" to "Mr."
Pg. 71	Penelope's last speech: change "American" to "Canadian."

Pg. 73   Roland's third speech: change "Ah, si...si, querida... more, more!" to "Ah, oui, oui, chérie, encore, encore!"

Pg. 73   Penelope's last speech: change "the Congressman" to "Mr. Bream."

Pg. 74   Whiting's fourth speech: change "Congressman" to "Mr."

Pg. 75   Roland's second speech: in the second parenthetical direction, change "Hispanic" to "French," then replace the entire speech with the following: "De problem wit de P.U. process is dat it always took more henergy to produce de fuel dan de fuel produced hitself. Finally, Doctor Zingel found a way around dis 'urdle and solved de problème."

Pg. 75   Whiting's third speech: change "Congressman" to "Mr." and change "Speedy Gonzales" to "Céline Dion."

Pg. 75   Whiting's fourth speech: change "Congressman" to "Mr. Bream."

Pg. 78   Roland's first speech: change "Oh si...si, querida" to "Oh oui, oui chérie..."

Pg. 79   Lorena's third speech: change "señor" to "monsieur."

Pg. 81   Lorena's first speech: change "Dios mio" to "Mon dieu."

Pg. 82   Mandy's fourth speech: change "the Congressman's" to "Mr. Bream's."

Pg. 84   Sharkey's fourth speech: change "Congressman" to "Mr."

Pg. 85   Penelope's last speech: change "a Maryland" to "an Ontario."

Pg. 87   Sharkey's last speech: change "President" to "Prime Minister."

Pg. 87   Gill's last speech: change "Madam President!" to "Prime Minister!"

Pg. 89   Josée's (Lorena's) first speech: change "Madam President!" to "Prime Minister!"

Pg. 89 José's (Lorena's) third speech: change "The Congressman" to "Mr. Bream."

Pg. 90 Gill's first speech: change "Department" to "Ministry."

Pg. 91 Gill's first speech: change "Madam President" to "Prime Minister."

Pg. 91 Sharkey's last speech: change "Madam President" to Prime Minister."

Pg. 93 Weever's first speech: change "President" to "Prime Minister."

Pg. 93 Josée's (Lorena's) last speech: change "Madam President" to "Prime Minister."

Pg. 94 Whiting's first speech: change "President" to "Prime Minister."

Pg. 94 Whiting's fourth speech: change "inauguration" to "throne speech."

Pg. 94 Whiting's last speech: change "Madame President' to "Prime Minister."

Pg. 94 Josée's (Lorena's) second speech: change "Congressman?" to "Mr. Bream?"

Pg. 95 Josée's (Lorena"s) fifth speech: change "Oh Dios mio. Te lo estoy diciendo..." to "Oh mon dieu. Je te le dis..."

Pg. 96 Bream's first speech: change "Dime algo en español" to "Dis-moi quelque chose en français."

Pg. 96 Josée's (Lorena's) first speech: change "Ah, ¿tu también? ¡Es increible!" to "Ah, toi aussi? C'est incroyable!"

Pg. 96 Josée's (Lorena's) second speech: change "¡Suficiente! ¡No es buen momento!" to "Assez! Ce n'est pas le bon temps!"

Pg. 96 Roland's first speech: change "Si, si." to "Oui, oui."

Pg. 97 Roland's first speech: replace "make me Secretary of State" to "appoint me to the Senate."

Pg. 97 Penelope's last speech: change "President of the United States" to "Prime Minister of Canada," and "Congressman" to "Mr."

Pg. 98 Bream's first speech: change "President" to "Prime Minister."